THE GIRL AND THE FERRYMAN

ERNST WIECHERT

The Girl and the Ferryman

Pilot Press · Publishers · New York · 1947

TRANSLATED FROM THE GERMAN BY

EITHNE WILKINS AND ERNST KAISER

Printed in the United States of America

Design by W. V. Eckardt

THE GIRL AND THE FERRYMAN

»» Chapter One ««

THE DYING WOMAN'S VOICE IS LOW, but so sharp that the guttering candle beside the bed flickers continually. The breath which carries her voice is already laborious, but it will not cease until she has said everything. Her hands lie side by side on the counterpane with the blue pattern. They are already the color of the next world. They are motionless, but the fingers still rise one by one and press down again into the faintly rustling cloth, as though adding up a list of debts.

The ferryman, Jürgen Doskocil, looks neither into the dying face nor at the moving fingers. He sits bent forward on the wooden stool, his heavy hands helpless in the empty space before his knees. Only his huge shoulders and the wild shock of hair on his bowed head can be seen. But he hears the movement of the fingers, writing figure after figure into the blue cloth. He knows they write wrongly, that even the death of this, his wife, is wrong, but he does not move a limb of his body. He folds himself up as if the heaviness of his limbs could protect his heart, toward which the cold words are aimed and the cold reckoning of the dying hands.

He knows that it will pass. He knows that everything passes: hunger, and shivering sleep, long nights of fishing in the black water, the children's mockery at his bulky shape, and the seasons as well as the years of his life, which sink heavily into the dark like the links of a boat-chain.

"A bear, that's what you looked like," the low, sharp voice murmurs. "And you were like a bear that creeps through the bushes. Did you ever bring me anything from market? Did you ever take me to the dancing? Did you ever buy me a ring?"

Five hours sleep I had, the ferryman thinks, *the whole five years—living on dry bread—*

"You wanted children from me, one every year, so that they should look like you and dogs would bark when they went by—" the voice goes on, and the finger presses again into the blue cloth.

If a man comes home, Jürgen thinks, *out of the cold water, out of the rain and the bad wind—and there's a toy there, all warm and small, that he can lift up with one hand—*

"And after I had borne it," the voice goes on, "you

didn't look at it—until it died in this mist and damp that creeps in right up to the hearth."

Three months after we came from the altar, Jürgen thinks, *and it wasn't mine, and they laid a stag's antlers at my door—*

"Say something!" the voice goes on. "Can't you hear?"

Now the ferryman lifts his gray and heavy face. It looks like a stone from the forests on the moor, as if the rain had been falling on it for forty long years. It is a face of bark, and no one knows what is underneath. No hand has ever come to lay it bare. Only the eyes shine out of its depths—eyes that have seen much.

"It isn't right to die like this," Jürgen Doskocil says softly.

He does not say it threateningly. He does not even say it accusingly. But now it is as though the mention of death had changed the air in the room. The woman's talking is blotted out, the candle burns with a motionless flame, and beyond the low, open window the water can be heard as it sinks below the wood of the ferry with dark, furtive sounds. An early moth whirs round the light. Jürgen would like to get up, to take it in his big hand and carry it outside as he usually does, but he dreads the sound of his heavy footsteps. *And perhaps it's Death,* he thinks.

And then the circling flight comes to an end with a hiss. A dark shadow falls on the wall and the flame twists to and fro, sizzling as though under damp wood. And then the wan light is motionless again.

But it seems as though someone has been there—a

strange breath, a strange glance—and gone away again, to return in his own time.

"It's not over yet," the woman's voice says. But this voice too is different now, neither more kind nor more malicious, but more remote as though further back in the changeless room. And although it has not become lower, Jürgen bends forward a little. "And even afterwards it won't be over," the voice says, "not even afterwards—"

Jürgen knows what she means. For he has had second sight ever since he can remember. Everybody knows that, and their scorn has been harder to bear than the burden of this gift which opens doors into the dark other world. He knows that she means to come again.

A faint breeze passes through the reeds outside and murmurs along the banks. Slowly his thoughts stir, walk down to the black water and stop there, heavily. The nets are lying in the lake; and the field must be plowed. There are rain, wind, and long distances to walk in wet clothes. There is the mockery of the children and the hatred between the two villages, the one on his side of the lake which they call the green village, and the other over on the moor which they call the black one. And he is between them, the only way, a shaky bridge over which walk bleeding feet. And now his hearth will be cold—and in the shadow will stand a wraith—

Someone is on his way, he thinks. He knows when someone is coming to strike the rusty plowshare on this side or on the other of the ferry crossing. He wakens in the night before the dark metallic clangor comes over the water. He has a ferryman's conscience, as the pastor says.

He lifts his head and listens. The reeds are still and only the water moves under the willow roots. Out of the shadow across his forehead he glances towards the bed. The woman's eyes are wide open in her white face, but they look beyond him out through the little window, and beyond that window there must be a vast space.

He wants to ask her whether he should read something out of the Bible, perhaps the Psalm about the wings of the morning, but it takes a long time for a word to rise from his soul and cross his lips. And now, when it has come the whole way to the gate of the mouth, the still air is shattered by the heavy waves of an iron shout from the other side of the water. A hand has struck the plowshare a single blow with the iron cudgel, and in the motionless silence each separate vibration resounds in Jürgen's ears. He loves the mighty gravity of this sound that rolls, strangely and almost threateningly, over the countryside, unrelated to wind or water or the light call of human voices, but like a bell from a dark tower. *Perhaps on Judgment Day it'll call like that,* Jürgen thinks, *when every other call is blotted out.*

"Fetch over," the woman says.

Her eyes are closed and her face is averted. Her voice has withdrawn still further into the unknown and it seems as if she repeats only in dream words she used to say harshly and admonishingly, when Jürgen still lay quietly under his blanket, alert before the call had come but hearkening until the iron's last echo had died down.

The sounds have died away, and Jürgen rises. Someone waits out there in the dark night. He knows nothing of him. Perhaps his eyes are turned towards the dim light here, and perhaps the summoning hand is once more hidden in the cloak. That is all Jürgen knows. For every time he goes to meet a secret. And some time Christ might be standing there, on his way to a dying man—and some time it might be God. *I have bethought me of it, Jürgen Doskocil*, he might say, *and I will give thee a field and a calm lake, where thou shalt no longer labor thus hard. Have thy rest now, my servant Doskocil*—

"Fetch over," the woman says again.

Jürgen takes the keys of the boat chain and the heavy oar from the back of the hearth. His feet are wrapped in rags and he moves out of the room like a heavy, silent animal. In the passage he lights the lantern, and he closes the door quietly.

The night opens before him like a warm vault. He feels the heavy cloud of the sky and smells the earth in which spring is awakening. From behind the black village a bird calls over the moor. It calls like something forgotten. The water murmurs under the hulk of the ferry, and a strange hand stirs the reeds.

Jürgen's shadow sways like the shadow of a tree and the tall grasses look false and evil in the white light of the lantern. As though in a lighted globe he walks through the night, and the globe moves slowly down to the water. If it were to sink there would be a faint hissing sound, like the moth in the candle flame. The chain clatters against the wood of the boat and the lantern throws a white brilliance into the dark mirror round the boat. Then the reeds rustle round the gliding hull, and there is only the whisper of water under the shallow keel.

They might be fooling me again, Jürgen thinks. *They've done it often enough—from the black village—running away when I come—but this was a real call—it sounds different when they do it—Christ might be coming to her—to her wicked death—*

In front of his eyes there is only a black wall which silently opens before him. But he senses the bank, as he feels the coming rain or the water growing shallow. For inanimate things are familiar to him, and only man builds the wall of strangeness between heart and heart.

The keel runs gently aground, and with his oar Jürgen steadies the boat in the current.

"Who is there?" he asks.

The earth is silent. An invisible eddy turns in the current, sinks beneath the boat, and is gone. The bird calls again from across the moor. A breath of wind comes out of the alder wood, touches the grass, and dies. The boat is quite alone.

"Is nobody there?" Jürgen asks.

He takes the lantern and steps ashore. He is not afraid, but his eyes are heavy as though with the second sight. He lifts the lantern close up to the plowshare. Dew lies pearly on the dark rust. No spot on it shows that a hand has struck it with the cudgel. He remains standing beside the gray wooden scaffolding and looks across the water towards the light by the dying woman's head.

'It might have been the boys from the black village,'

he thinks. 'They leave no tracks, like the cats from the woods.' And then he draws a deep breath and rows back. His thoughts lose themselves in the streaming water, and he has to row the boat upstream along the bank, because it has drifted down with the current to where the dead oak stands among the pines.

He enters quietly, for he knows what has happened. The white face is still warm, but under the skin the cold is slowly rising. Between the eyelids is a narrow slit, through which one looks deep down into the wells of death. The forefinger of the right hand is still slightly crooked from writing the last figure in the list of debts.

Jürgen closes the cool lids over the strangeness of death and smooths the fingers. And beyond that he does not know what to do about this death. Again he sits on the stool, his head sunk in his hands, staring into the shadow at the back of the hearth. He does not look at the silent face, for it does not belong to him. He has suffered much from it throughout five years. He knows his spade and his plow, his oar and his boat. But this was something he never knew, something that entered his life like a strange stone striking his heart and falling off again. The child that she bore was strange, and so was the womb that had borne it and the mouth that wrangled with him. She had fooled him, as they all fooled him. "Fetch over!" But then it slipped away through the night, and he was nothing but the bridge over which they all walked.

At dawn he washes the body, clothes it in the shroud and covers the face with a shawl. He keeps his eyes shut

When the shadow of the roof touches the boat's bows, he knows there are five more hours until sunset. He strikes the hanging plowshare twice. That is the signal for Heini, and after a while he appears. He comes along the green path between forest and marsh, a willow wand in his hand, not looking to right or left, obedient and humble as a dog. He is the bastard child of a woman who works in the forest — sixteen years old, he is as twisted as a willow tree. His face is ancient, with features other than human. Shut, cold, with long eyelashes, a face turned inwards, all by itself, like the quiet faces of mushrooms. When he lifts his lashes, only then his brown eyes glow gently and childlike, bright from within. Jürgen once freed him from a trap which the forester had set deep in the marsh. Mute, without complaint, like an animal, he had sat in it for twenty-four hours, through day and night. Since then he comes whenever the iron calls twice.

"Have to plow, Heini," Jürgen says.

Heini nods. He looks towards the sheet across the window. When Jürgen says nothing he goes in. Jürgen sets the plow to the edge of the little field and lays the wide harness around his chest. 'A horse,' he thinks, standing there waiting without impatience, looking towards the forest. 'In five years perhaps there'll be a horse — but life goes on without it, too.'

Heini comes back without speaking, only his face is uneasy, as if he had stolen something.

And then Jürgen throws his weight against the harness and plows the first furrow through the black earth. From far away it looks as though an animal had reared up,

as he undresses the body, for it does not belong to him, and even beyond death the law of chastity prevails.

Then he nails the coffin together in the shed where he keeps the nets. The boards are of planed spruce and they smell of summer and the forest. He has no money for a black coffin, and these boards are clean. No hand but his has touched them on the way from tree to coffin.

When the sun rises over the hazy forest he sits on the sawing jack in front of the shed, eating his black bread and drinking the cold coffee from the hearth. 'The nets,' he thinks, 'and then to the pastor and to the office — I can take the fish with me and sell them — the grave digger gets ten pounds — the bearers get five — I must get a loaf — and in the afternoon call Heini for the plowing — time for the potatoes — spread the nets in the creek by the rushes — up to the last the fingers were crooked — get the bownets ready — market day tomorrow — stay at the ferry — cut seed potatoes — who will come to me in my trouble?'

The pair of finches from last summer are here again, sitting by his feet and waiting for crumbs out of his hand. A comforting bond reaches back from them to summer, which will come again with its thunderstorms over the forest. The fish rise for an abundant catch when summer lightning flashes over the lake. And he will catch young animals again in the forest, look into their moist eyes and stroke their quivering skin. Animals are better than children. They have no mockery and they cannot talk about him behind his back.

As he walks to the boat, with the oar in his hand, he

looks like an animal from the moorland forest. The dark hair falls over the gray face, the shoulders cast a shadow like a tree, the legs are bent. When he takes the chain from the post, he sees his face in the murky water. He keeps his hands still and bends down towards it. That other one looks at him, looming out of the depths, a stranger. He does not know what he looks like, and he is startled. He knows work, sorrow and want, but he knows nothing of his face. He knows of his hands and the heaviness of his limbs, of his strength and of his soundless tread. But his mouth? It does not speak and it does not smile. What is his mouth for? What are cheeks and forehead for? In his life his face lies as a stone lies in the forest. Only the eyes reach deep down into his heart: sad eyes like those of an old wolf; eyes that have second sight, seeing things far beyond the world. He turns round quickly and looks towards the cottage. But the sheet hangs across the window, and on the oak over the gray roof the finch sits. When he looks down again, the chain has moved, and the picture, broken up, sinks into the depths.

At midday he is back again. Everything has been made ready, and the pastor has promised that the bells will ring. He does it for nothing. "You are the child of my congregation, Doskocil," he often says, "God's most faithful servant – on your shoulders you carry a heavy load."

'It is good that they will ring,' Jürgen thinks on his way home. 'It's only a white coffin, but for the bells they open the gate up there. The poor must speak up – and the children are going to sing – for it's not for me.'

Round the bend the cottage comes into sight. Sunshine lies over the forest, which is coming into leaf. The goat on the paddock lifts its head and looks in his direction. Yes, death is like a furrow on the water and to right and to left everything goes on its dark way. On the left bank the children from the black village sit fishing. "Doskocil!" a clear young voice calls out. "Doskocil can't d this – gets a child that isn't his –"

Jürgen sees the laughing faces. 'Who will give childr to me?' he thinks. '*They* wouldn't sing like that.' F rows past without answering, but his arms are tired a the sun is cold on water and land.

He glances once into the twilit room. The air is c over the white shape, and the room is like a strange h into which he looks at night. All things there are se and look at him like enemies. He is not guilty, he is alive, but this has gained power over the room sin has been away. Death is more than a furrow. The still, with a different smell. The breath of his own here has been wiped away as from a dimmed mirr has shared with another, and the other has taken hi as well, in a cunning game. More than the woman h here. Something of the room has died too – a piec hearth, the security of the floor boards, somethin roof's darkness. Yes, death is more than a furrow

He cooks a few whitings in an earth hole li stones, and meanwhile prepares the coffin. He ha but wood shavings and sawdust. Over it he rough white cloth. Towards evening he will twigs to decorate the rim.

walking on its hind legs, laboriously keeping its balance. And the too long arms behind him, which hold the handles of the plow, might be a keeper's cautious gesture, trying to prevent the unnaturally erect creature from tumbling.

They both look down at the earth, and the earth is curiously near to them, because they see every span of ground with every blade of grass and every stone for the last time, before the shining plowshare turns it down to the dark; and because there is no intermediary between them and the earth, no yoke of oxen, no horse. For both of them it is as if they were lifting each clod with their own bodies. Heini still holds the willow wand in his hand. He does not think of cracking it like a whip, but for him there would be something incomplete about the picture in which he moves if it were missing.

Only when they turn the plow for the first time and stop, breathing deeply, before the new furrow, he says, with his eyes turned towards the cottage: "A cold stove — that's what people are like — " and Jürgen has to look at him for a while, with his dark brows drawn into a painful frown, before he nods in place of an answer.

They plow until it is time to make a break for coffee. Both are breathing hard, and only now and then, when they turn the plow, does a word fall like a stone from a tired hand. "The buzzard's there," or "They're going to ring the bells," or "There are two pike for you in the boat."

When they are drinking the cold coffee out of a blue tin pot and breaking the black bread in their hands, they have a talk. They sit on the warm grass bank beside the plow. They look out over the gleaming horizon, and the sun lies in slanting blue beams over the rim of cloud.

"The woodpecker was calling, this morning," Heini says.

"Yes, it means rain when he calls."

"What did you say? What does he do with the mandrake?"

Jürgen looks aside, towards the silent forest. "He carries it on Friday—when the moon is waxing."

"Can you see it?"

"Sometimes."

"Inside a hollow tree?"

"Yes."

"It gives you all the treasures there are?"

"Grandfather used to say so."

"And also—also makes you straight again?"

"He said so."

The boy clasps his long, hunchback's hands round his knees and looks out over the moor. His eyes are open wide, and the sun wakes golden dots in the gentle brown of the iris. Jürgen sighs and stretches out his legs for his knees are trembling from the strain of plowing. "We must manage," he says quietly. "If they didn't have us they would torment the dogs."

Heini nods. He even smiles. "You are stronger than all of them together," he says. "That makes it not so hard—"

When the sun goes down they have finished. Jürgen fetches the pike from the boat. "Thanks," he says, as he gives them to the boy. Then he rows out with his three-fold fixed nets.

It is growing dark when he returns but he can smell the fir twigs the hunchback has laid on the threshold, a thickly woven wreath and a small heap of green branches. As he opens the door his strong hands tremble. He puts the two stools in their places. Then he lights the lamp and waits, holding his breath, until the light has spread over the bed, the walls, and the hearth. Nothing has changed, but everything is rigid; the outline of the body, the air, the whole room. Death fills his house, and he himself feels frozen like a reed in the ice of the lake. There are stronger things than his strength, and it is terrible when a human being grows rigid. Plowing goes on, and fishing, but this will always remain. A death never goes away. Never does anyone die all by himself and for himself alone—Heini might be there, or perhaps a small animal—just a little, warm animal.

Then within the shed he lifts the coffin onto his shoulders and carries it into the room. The coffin is lighter than death. Before he lifts the body he looks around, but no one is here except his shadow.

When he has milked the goat, he stays on the stool for a while longer. The goat turns her head and searches with snuffling lips for the pocket in his gray jacket. And he lays his forehead on the animal's warm back, which smells of grass and sun and the strange life of a strange creature.

A late cart clatters along the forest track. The echo runs with it, rattling and grinding. The whole forest is awake, resounding and calling, moving along with the cart.

Jürgen is already standing at the ferry, so that the iron may not ring loudly through the forest. It is somebody from the other side of the moor.

"The wife's dead?" a voice asks out of the dark, after the water is moving under the ferry.

"Yes," Jürgen says.

"Hard without a wife," the voice says after a while. And again only the eddies ripple under the joints in the wood.

Two coins clink against one another, and then the night moves off again resounding and calling. The light on the ferry goes out and the pulley groans over the cable. Wild ducks are piping under the stars as Jürgen goes to the shed, to sleep there on the wood shavings.

Next day the funeral takes place. The green village buries the dead woman, but the black village also follows the coffin. For an hour death blots out the gesture of hatred. The pastor looks as though he had just been fetched from the plow and had thrown a surplice around his shoulders. His hands are brown and heavy, and Jürgen feels at rest and at home with these hands whose gesture moves over the open grave like a sower's hand over the field. Jürgen feels that the pastor is giving a queer sermon, but in his words too he feels at home. For the pastor preaches of Samson, the servant of the Lord, and with his heavy tired mind Jürgen grasps that there, too, there had been something about a woman—perhaps this passage of the Bible might be a little hard on the dead woman under the bright spruce boards. But when he lifts his eyes to the pastor's face, he knows that everything is kept well and justly there: the fate of both the living and the dead.

"Much have you fetched over in your life, Jürgen Doskocil, you faithful ferryman," the pastor says, "the green and the black, life and death. And your oar was true, as your coin was true. And when Death was coming to your house, you went and fetched him over, faithful and obedient, as though a child in its weakness had called for you. This will be accounted unto you for righteousness, you faithful ferryman. And she who will knock at God's door will tell of your faithfulness, for what dims our eyes will then have fallen away from her."

Jürgen thinks of his little field as he throws earth onto the coffin, and of the corn he cut together with the dead woman before anger had moved her heart against him. And the third handful of earth he throws down to her feet, as if to raise her out of the shroud, and he knows that what the pastor says of the resurrection is true.

The school children sing, with long drawn notes, and the women's voices float high and mournful over the dragging melody.

Jürgen still stands beside the pastor at the mound, and he feels how good it is that he need not speak. "And if she comes again, Doskocil," the pastor says, "remember always, they rise from our souls and not out of the grave. And one should not forbid them to stay and dwell with us. But now you must take someone into your house, that you may have a plate on the table and a human voice in your heart."

"There is the goat," Jürgen says.

But the pastor shakes his head and looks over his congregation, to see whether the villages have already separated. "Not one of these," he adds. "Perhaps someone will call, as happened that night. Then ferry over and see if God has sent you something."

The bells cease chiming as Jürgen goes to the ferry. The sky is empty and he treads softly, as if he were walking through a sleeping house. When from afar he sees the goat beside the cottage his breath grows easier in his heavy breast.

He ferries over the mourners from the village on the moor and refuses the money, saying: "Thank you kindly."

He puts his gray jacket on again, makes the nets ready, stands a long time on the doorstep and then at last goes in. The room is still silent. But now the air has a faint smell of lake and forest, and when he passes his hand over the clay hearth there is a trace of sunshine on it, falling through the little window.

It is beginning to darken when he comes home from the water. He has much to think about. He milks the animal and shakes up the straw. He cuts potatoes for seeding and hammers away at a chain for the fish box. And when he goes into the house, for a piece of wire that hangs at the back of the hearth, he has forgotten the strangeness that has not yet passed from time and space. A cool wind goes over him as he opens the door, and even before he can realize that he has made the draught, he sees her sitting by the hearth. Only the outlines show in the failing light, the curve of forehead and shoulders, and her eyes and hands directed at something invisible, far away from him, without question or threat. Then before the image has filled his mind, it flickers in the dust, is gone again, fades out as though behind a closing door, without a trace.

Jürgen nods to himself once, in the empty room. Then he goes to the hearth for the wire. He has to reach for it twice before his hand grips it. He finishes the chain, but he goes back to the goatshed, hangs the lantern on the post and works there, pausing now and then to listen to the animal nibbling its evening fodder.

This night he sleeps by the hearth.

»» Chapter Two ««

ON THE MEADOWS BETWEEN THE TWO villages the first hay had been mown, and the air was sweet with the scent of withering stalks. The corncrake shouted the whole night long, and an hour after the constellations had passed the meridian, the cuckoo began to call in the oak over Jürgen's cottage. Then Jürgen awoke from his cautious sleep, as an animal wakes at the first breath of dawn, and looked towards the hearth to see if he were alone. Seldom did that pale image rise out of the depths of sleep. It seemed that the soul must be filled with thoughts of the day before it could cause that slight shadow in the half light of dusk, existing without demand or resistance or threat, only to fade away upon the start of remembrance.

Then Jürgen got up in the dim light of white nights, made a fire on the hearth and drank the hot coffee on the doorstep of his cottage. Mist still lay on the water, a dog barked in the black village and received a furious response from the other side, as though the hatred of man had also spread among the animals. But the breath of the earth still hovered immaculate over the world; in the northeast a gateway had already opened up, white, over the forest, and Jürgen knew that the sun was rising. 'The dead are abroad,' he thought, 'and the living do not mean me well, but the sun is coming. Grass grows, and the fish go into the nets—the sun is good, and he gives to everything its own shadow.'

It took a long time for this thought to unfold in his mind, but in it lay comfort and the quiet peace with which he began his day's work. He was still smoking his short pipe filled with dried clover, and the little glow between his hands was like a warming fireside for him, belonging to him alone, not threatened by any shadow or dangerously distorted by any twilight.

Then with his dragnet he rowed out into the rushy creeks, or took the scythe and went to his patch of meadow within the forest.

But in the evenings, in the floating light, the faint anxiety of dusk hovered again before each footstep.

Together with Heini he had stacked the hay into ricks, and the sun had gone down behind the black forest. They sat with their backs against the warm grass and looked across to where the deer stepped, red and shy, out of the darkening bushes.

"There's no net for the dead," Jürgen said, striking a light in his hollowed hand with flint and tinder, "the way there is for fish or beasts—you can't catch them so that they aren't there any more, and so they're always there—"

Heini turned his old, child's face a little to one side, to where the wall of the forest jutted out, a dark wedge, into the clearing, but then he looked straight ahead again. He had lost all sense of fear in the shadow of this man who talked with the dead. His long fingers were tying knots in a green stalk. "I've read that they used to walk in the old times, too," he answered. "They had to change their graves and heap stones on top of them, in a big field."

But Jürgen shook his head. "Conscience walked, an evil one—in those times—but with her it's different. I still owe her something, and now she wants it."

"And the mandrake?" Heini asks softly.

"No, not for that."

"I saw him yesterday," Heini went on. "On his oak. But he had nothing in his beak. I climbed up, but there was only rotten wood in the hole and empty nutshells from a squirrel. And he laughed at me from back in the forest. He laughs like the children when they've thrown a stone at my back."

Jürgen nodded. "He has a red crest, and some says he's the devil of the forest—but no one knows if the soul is the same as the garment."

"There's such a lot to know, Doskocil—such a lot."

And again they fell silent, and only the little fire

glowed in Jürgen's pipe, with a faint sizzling when he drew in his breath.

A week later, the day before midsummer's day, Jürgen went to town with his fish. The stars still stood high in the sky, and for three hours the heavy boat glided alongside forest, meadows and moor. Jürgen sold his fish, keeping back only three bundles of tench. When he lifted them out of the water in the stern of the boat, he looked for a while at their helplessly opening and shutting gills, and then went into the shop by the river, where he was known. He laid the fish down by the counter and stepped back quietly into the background, as though it were not nearly his turn yet.

"Fine fish, Master Doskocil?" the shopkeeper asked amiably.

"Caught this morning," Jürgen answered, stepping back a little further into the shadow. "But there's no hurry."

When the last customer stood at the cash desk Jürgen came out of his corner, handed the fish over the counter and asked, so quietly that the merchant had to bend forward, if he could have a colored kerchief and a ring in exchange for them. A small ring, perhaps with a red stone, the sort that was worn in the villages.

The merchant hid his astonishment, reckoned quickly with half-closed eyes and then said that of course it would be all right. Only a gold wedding ring, of course, he couldn't get for that. But a little ring, oh yes, that could be managed.

Just such a little ring would do, Jürgen said. He

searched long and carefully with his fingers that were slightly bent from the water, put a red and white patterned kerchief aside, and after a while kept one of the small rings in the palm of his hand, one which gave out a feeble, artificial gleam from a red glass stone. It looked like a child's ring in his hand. He tied it up in a checked handkerchief, asking if he still owed anything, then said a word of thanks and went to the door with lowered eyes, his cap in his hand.

"Good luck!" the shopkeeper said and smiled benevolently.

Jürgen turned round once more, looked at him with melancholy eyes and answered quietly: "It's not for this life."

While he was making the boat ready, a child watched him, motionless, its hands clasped round a rusty hoop with which it had been playing. Its fair hair was tied into a little pigtail, and its eyes followed every movement in the boat, like the eyes of a little dog waiting for the moment to start.

Jürgen looked around carefully and put the chain right once more, although nothing was wrong with it.

"Would you like to come along?" he asked at last, reddening before the little human creature that did not retreat at his question.

"I'll make you a cushion here in the stern and buy you a bun—"

No answer.

"I've a house by the lake, and the cuckoo calls all day long, and blue dragonflies sit in the reeds—"

Not even the pupils of the eyes flickered. They were wide open, like a well into which words, movements and gestures sank.

"We'll drink coffee and goat's milk, and I'll catch a squirrel for you, and a blue roller—"

When nothing happened, no sound, no motion of the little brown hands, Jürgen gave it up. For a while yet he kept the boat steady in the current with his oar, then he let it glide downstream, his face still turned back. And at the moment when the river began to bear him away, the enchantment of the bank snapped.

"*Water-bogie!*" the child called in a high, clear voice, set its hoop rolling and ran along the bank. The clatter of the iron on the cobblestones awoke a loud, threatening echo that reached out over the water, and the clear voice struck like a bird's cry at the gray figure that was crouching down like an owl in the boat, as though to escape the hurtful cry. "Water-bogie!—Water-bogie!"

All the way home Jürgen's eyes were fixed on the bundle lying on the seat, in which the kerchief and the ring were wrapped up.

There were no midsummer celebrations on St. John's Night in the two villages, and so, in the light of the stars and the northerly shimmer of the white night, the gray figure looked like that of a crouching animal, silently busy at the grave mound on which the shadows of the forest still lay. No spade struck against a stone, only the hands quietly lifted the earth until a deep hollow was dug into the mound. There rose a breath of all that is hidden in the moist earth, and a withered smell of rotting wreaths clung round the little hill. Then there was the slight rustling sound of a knotted piece of cloth being undone, a faint shimmer as of dull metal shone once, and then the hands were filling the earth into the hole again, carefully, as though they were dropping it onto a face grown still, instead of onto the folds of a red kerchief in which a tiny ring was hidden.

Jürgen remained kneeling, leaning his hands on the ground, his eyes still fastened on the heap that rose up, dark and rounded, out of the smooth sand. "If I owed something," he said softly, "I'm willing to pay—I never brought a kerchief from market: here is a kerchief—I never brought a ring from the town: here is the ring—a child was what I wanted in my house, but it was frightened of me and laughed at me—I can't help it— Take those other things and go to sleep now—don't come again— Wear the kerchief and put the ring on your hand—It's hard enough seeing through water right to the bottom where the stones lie, and to talk to the fish that open their gills. Leave it at that, all will be well—and sleep in peace—Jesus Christ help you with His Blood and all that has power in heaven and on earth and under the earth— Amen."

He listened for an answer from the bottom of the grave, but only a faint breeze stirred in the trees of the forest, and a water bird called from far over the river. But when he lifted his head and stood up soundlessly from his kneeling position, over the wall of the forest a star shot down out of the pale heights, cleaving a shining rift through the infinite vault, and fell, fading out, behind the treetops.

Jürgen did not think of anything while it fell. Never had his thoughts moved so fast that he could form a wish between the beginning and the end of such a luminous track. But the warmth of some comfort and a promise rose slowly within him long after the sight had vanished and the white night had closed again over the fleeting trace.

He left the graveyard, avoided the village and walked along the edge of the forest back to his cottage. When he opened his fingers and shut them again, he still felt some loose grains of sand on the palms of his hands.

⋙ ⋘

In the same hour when the shooting star passed over the graveyard, half a mile back in the forest two human paths crossed, touching each other and parting after an hour's common journey which linked their uncharted strangeness. Yet the momentarily knotted bond of their destinies was cast in a natural way round the ferryman's cottage.

One of these ways walked Mathias Südekum, tailor from the black village. He walked it in a curious manner, zigzagging between the trees on the left and the trees on the right, as though they were rolling him to and fro like a ball. He walked it, too, in dazed awareness that this was not the right way, that his feet were obeying an unknown law and that his head was not capable of keeping proper control over those subordinate and now rebellious members, his feet. And therefore from the narrow forest track his voice rose continually, exhorting, threatening, admonishing or pleading, towards the white strip of sky which hung over him in a ghostly, unchanging manner; and therefore he raised the iron ell he carried with him like a sword over a hesitantly following army, or sometimes like a cross against the dark advance of some heathen or spectral horde.

Mathias Südekum, tailor from the village on the moor, no native of these parts and a bitter scorner of the people and the countryside in which he was now living, was far from being what, around the moor, a tailor was commonly imagined to be: a physically wretched creature, unfit for heavy work and therefore humble and a laughing stock. On the contrary, in his tall gaunt body lay a dread strength, crouching in somber, derisive silence, which in everyday life at fittings made him cast the coarse material over angular peasant limbs with disdainful gestures, until once every season this strength broke out unexpectedly, and after homeric speeches hurled itself jubilantly into ruthless brawling, which cleared the inn in the green village as well as in the black. This was done for the reason smilingly stated in retrospect, that 'the backs one generally just fits clothes on are something one should know right down to the skin.'

Mathias Südekum, blessed with a wife who now and then scalded him with boiling water, and with six children whose names he forgot from time to time, was dissatisfied with the midsummer celebrations which he had intended for his own honor. He had been sitting in the tavern of the forest village, his ell on the table in front of him, and had made one of his inspiring speeches to the forest people.

"You blindworms," he had said in his flowery manner, "the time has come again for Mathias Südekum to tread somewhat on your tails, so that you may return into the swamp from which your mothers spewed you forth. Presumptuous you have become, my swampy friends, and have forgotten to swing your caps down to your knees when you meet me. Presumptuous your toads of children have become, who throw stones at me from behind the hedges, when I honor the village with my presence. Presumptuous your womenfolk have become, who take off their skirts when they come to me for a fitting, and who all stink, because they only wash at Christmas—"

Here the first beer mug came flying and was answered with masterly aim; but Czwallina, the inn keeper, had appeared with his wolfhound, which the gendarme had talked him into having so that the charges on account of assault and battery might become less frequent, and so nothing had come of it. Südekum hated dogs with green shimmering eyes, and so he had not been able to do anything but drench the whole crowd of his enemies in the acid of his scorn and to land the juice of his chewing-plug into the detested faces, right across the table. For he was an expert in long shots of this kind, and no growling wolfhound was capable of stopping this fire or diverting it from its precisely determined course.

But there had been no actual fisticuffs. The enemy,

rich in bitter experience, had withdrawn from the field with sullen threats, and the only thing in which Südekum succeeded was slapping a few faces, slaps which he, moving his table to the door, had distributed as a hasty gesture of farewell. But this heroism that met with no resistence had not satisfied him, and when he left the tavern, the last to go, hoping that in the darkness of the night the battle that was due him would yet flare up, he had stumbled over a bucket filled with water which had been placed providently on the steps. It had been of no avail that he had roared like Polyphemus into the invisible laughter of his enemies. At last he had found his ell again, had taken the wrong road, and now moved, growling and resentful, on his staggering way, obscurely aware that battle and bed were lost for this night.

When the shooting star descended, which had filled the man at the grave with a promise of comfort, the tailor Südekum was coming out into a clearing that was strange to him, of which he only knew that it must be a long way from his house. He stared up after the shining streak long after it had vanished, trying to bring the phenomenon into its place in the misty flux of events through which he was drifting. "Magic!" he said loudly and disapprovingly. "Put a—spell on me—they have—the—folk down below are out tonight—squirt of plug in the sky—queer—"

And after laborious attempts he collapsed onto a tree stump overflowing with fresh resin, and sat there resting his head in his hands, looking broodingly up into the sky to see whether this apparition would occur again, contrary to all the laws of nature.

The second way under the high firmament of this night, lit by wandering lights, came the smallholder Michael Grotjohann, with his daughter Marte. He too had missed his way in this forestland he did not know, and some distance from the village lying further east he had got deeper and deeper into the thin mist and the darkening territory of the deep forest. He was deaf to his daughter's quiet warnings and certain that God would go before him as a pillar of fire, illuminating the way to the little farm of a relative where he hoped to find repose in the secure community of a new faith, after the pains and sorrows of manifold disaster in recent years.

For the smallholder Grotjohann had been "called to grace" at the beginning of spring, not by the pastor of his parish, whom he called an 'emissary of the powers of darkness,' but by a certain Mr. Maclean, an itinerant preacher of the Church of the Thousand Days domiciled in Salt Lake City, U. S. A., an ambassador of the Mormon state who was carrying out a zealous and successful campaign of conversion among the neglected parishes between forest and moor. His call to grace had preceded that of his daughter, who being a pretty and light-hearted girl, had passed through numerous adventures of pastoral love, before the somber and ascetic appearance of the Reverend Armstrong Maclean had changed her into a penitent Magdalen. Nor had her rather lazy, patient animal mind become conscious whether the mysterious symbols of the distant Golden City which she was to see in a year's time had plunged her into the sweetness of abandon to remorse, or the uncanny, always veiled and unrevealing eyes of the herald of those symbols.

Furthermore, the new faith, from which the rumor of notorious polygamy could not be separated, brought its believers scorn, hatred and persecution from the lesser authorities of State and Church. And a reputation for an amiably willing susceptibility to love still clung to Marte's person long after her call to grace, so that, when at night in her room she knelt in prayer together with the Reverend Maclean, more than once an impatient knocking had sounded at her window, and the missionary's somber eyes had peered into hers with a threatening query.

So Michael Grotjohann, after brooding for long weeks over the shining picture postcards of Salt Lake City, and making confused, profound, ecstatic speeches, had sold his farm out of hand, in order to 'exorcise himself in prayer' at the house of a cousin in the forest district, until he should become worthy of the journey to the Golden City, where according to his primitive belief, God, gold and loving women were waiting yearningly for his arrival. So, shortly before the beaten conqueror Mathias Südekum entered the clearing on his search for the right road and sleep, the smallholder in grace and his daughter were sitting in the shadow of a lime tree on the edge of a ditch, only separated by the breadth of the track from the tree stump on which the tailor, perplexed and full of gloomy intuition, sank down before their eyes.

His cloudy gaze, searching the darkness of the forest, could not be blamed for taking the hatless, entirely hairless head of the Mormon disciple for a mushroom or a piece of rotting, phosphorescent wood, any more than the smallholder could for taking the muttering figure, armed with an iron rod, for an emissary of hell, who had come out on midsummer's night in order to indulge in diabolical lewdness with lustful witches in an ill-famed glen. Only Marte, tired to death, thinking neither of the unholy night nor of the devil, but cooling her bare feet in what little dew there was at the bottom of the ditch, realized that here was a drunken man in search of his domestic hearth, and could not suppress a faint smile at the exhortatory gestures of the nocturnal apparition. She too saw the luminous track of the falling star and thought in dull uneasiness of midsummer's night the year before and her unholy experiences, and listened with a queer excitement in her tired blood, to the sad croaking of the toads in the depths of the forest, ceaseless as a bell tolling under the ground. On distant meadows a corncrake began its monotonous call, mist hung over the alder groves, and the bewitchment of the hour sank, tight and stupefying, over wanderers, way, and destination.

She did not know if she had been asleep, but she opened her eyes when her father, in sudden decision, strengthened by silent prayer, rose from the edge of the ditch and, with arms outstretched in conjuration, approached the cowering figure on the tree stump. "In the name of the Saint of the Thousand Days!" he began in his high-pitched, childish voice, "whoever you may be, on infamous paths, far from the streets of the Golden City—"

A yell interrupted him, echoing back a hundredfold from the resounding depths of the forest, a howl of mortal fear, and a rearing back before the hairless, bony skull that loomed up in front of Südekum's eyes as though out of the bowels of the earth.

"In the name of the Father—!" Mathias roared, flinging himself to one side, as though the bushes in the clearing would open up like the doors of a church and give him sanctuary. But the resin under the seat of his trousers, which had swollen luxuriantly under the June sun, held him back with a strength superior to that of his drunken limbs. With cold sweat on his forehead, he realized that he was under a spell such as otherwise happened only in dreams, when he was in the grip of a nightmare; and his helpless lips shaped delirious words, to reach the forecourts of grace before the outstretched bony arms could stamp the seal of death on his brow.

At this roaring and these cries of exhortation Grotjohann grew rigid, and so they both stopped in frozen attitudes, one with outstretched arms in the middle of the track, the other half fallen off his seat, his left hand on the wet grass to keep his body from tumbling over, and his right hand stretched with outspread fingers, towards the murderous specter which in the midst of an unknown forest, under spitting stars, far from wife and children, was about to plunge him into an unsanctified grave.

Then they both heard a sound of childlike laughter

welling up from an innocent breast, at first suppressed, then rising more and more freely into the bewitched silence. And when, at first only listening, not yet taking their horrified eyes from one another, but then furtively glancing towards the ditch, they both saw the figure of the girl leaning against the fir tree to support herself in the excess of her mirth, it seemed to both of them, the drunken man and the exorciser, that the harmless reality of earth must still somehow be there and that not all of the world could be submerged and distorted in ghostliness.

"Who are you, my poor brother?" Grotjohann asked first, with the form of address he had become accustomed to use since he received grace.

"Who are you calling brother?" Mathias answered, more struck by the queer form of address than by the fact that Death had begun to speak. "What devil led you here to frighten those who go their ways in peace? And why have you got no hair on your head, you ghost?"

After these introductory formulae, a technical conversation developed as to origins, way, destination and wandering, which Mathias concluded with the grandiose assurance that 'Master Jonathan together with his good lady' should slumber gently and safely within an hour under the blessed roof of his brother-believer.

Once more a peal of half suppressed merriment came from the other side of the ditch. Explanation followed as to the person of the daughter. There was a renewed, unsuccessful attempt on the part of the tailor to rise chivalrously from his seat, accompanied by muffled exhortations against deviltry, spells, nightmares, hobgoblins and the ghosts of the alder grove.

"It must be resin," Marte said, stepping out of the shadows onto the path.

Her appearance and this remark gave Mathias cause for long brooding. "If it's resin," he said at last, slowly, "I must take my trousers off."

"The devil reeks out of your mouth, brother," the smallholder remarked rebukingly, as they bent down to grasp his hands.

"Depravity shines from your bald head, brother," Mathias retorted.

When they had got him to his feet, he only made a grand gesture with his ell, looked up once searchingly at the stars, and then began to walk back along the way he had come. "Let's leave it," he said conclusively.

The trees were still strange to him, but a dim instinct, born of the fear of death he had experienced through this meeting, drove him forward like a startled animal on the way to its lair. The other two, faltering between fear and trust, tiptoed along behind him.

Was he quite certain about the way, they asked. It seemed to him he could smell the water, the tailor answered enigmatically. But they did not want to go to the water; the cousin lived in the forest. As the hart panted for cooling streams, so did his soul yearn for the waterman, Mathias cried out. The waterman knew all ways, including the way to the cousin, indeed to all the cousins there were. And who was the waterman, they asked. He was the man who talked with the dead.

Grotjohann turned around towards his daughter, but she only smiled as she had in the clearing. She was much too tired to be frightened.

When the forest opened with the oaks over Jürgen's cottage standing up into the white sky, Mathias knew he was home. "Come here, bald-head," he said, stopping, "can you see now that I know all the roads? Down there under the oaks is the waterman. And over yonder is the village of the blindworms who put a bucket in front of my feet, and bitterly shall they yet weep for it. Over there is the village of the frogs, and it's every bit as foul as the other one. And between the two of them there's the ferry, and the ferryman can carry a boat on his back all by himself. We don't love each other, but he is stronger than I am, and for that the devil take him too — "

"But he lives in the forest, brother!" Grotjohann cried in despair. "And he never wrote to me about a ferry."

Instead of an answer Mathias stretched forth his iron ell, laid its angle round Grotjohann's neck and pulled the resisting man close to his eyes, which still had a tendency to see single objects double. "You've a bad character, bald man," he said after scrutinizing the other's face. "Your nose is crooked, very crooked, and that's bad. The inn keeper down among the blindworms has a crooked nose, and that's why he has taken on a wolfish mongrel — bad, brother — who knows what sort of a cousin you have back in the forest — " And with that he let the resentfully struggling man go.

Jürgen had been sitting in the goatshed, rubbing the

groaning animal's belly, ever since his return. It had torn out the peg to which it was tethered on the paddock and had got among fresh clover. "You silly thing," he said softly, "what good has it done you? What am I going to do if you go away too—how stupid you all are—always thinking with your bellies. Does it hurt so much—yes—just a little while, you stupid—"

The cudgel thundered on the plowshare, as though announcing the Day of Judgment. Jürgen got up. Stars were dancing before his eyes from the strain, and his thoughts went back to the graveyard, as though perhaps it came from there. But he felt none of the faint chill which at other times came between heart and breath when the invisible became visible. So he went outside slowly.

Since he did not come, as expected, through the door of his cottage, but with his soundless tread round the corner of the house into their midst, the girl retreated with a little cry from the gray figure that suddenly appeared uncannily out of the uncanny earth.

"Don't be frightened," he said, "I was with the goat—she got into fresh clover—"

"Yes," the tailor said, "so here is bald-head. Just look at his nose. He wants to go to his cousin in the forest. He'll be calling you 'brother' any moment. And besides, he has a daughter who laughs when Death is at your throat. Will you bring them over to their 'cousin?' But first I want to cross over to the frogs."

Jürgen looked calmly from one to the other, but past the girl. "Where is it?" he asked Grotjohann.

"I'll set him over first," he then decided. "Sit you down at the hearth meanwhile."

They followed him with their eyes, as he forced the boat through the current. The water was white and blank where the Milky Way was reflected in it. Only the edges were black on each side. From the young birches came an overpowering smell, and everything looked as if no human voice had ever called from bank to bank. "It's like America," Grotjohann said thoughtfully.

When Jürgen came back, the cottage door was open, and he went quickly to the goatshed to see to the sick animal before he began the long journey once more.

"She's better now," the girl's dark voice said. "I think you can be easy."

She was kneeling beside the animal, looking up at him over her shoulder. He saw that she had picked some fresh leaves and that the animal was eating out of her hand.

"There's blessing in your hand," he answered, and had to speak more loudly in the middle of the sentence to stop his voice trembling. "Three hours I was with her, worrying, and now you come and it's all right."

"It's no thanks to my hand—you had pulled her through."

"But not everyone would have gone straight to the shed—and you're tired, too—"

She bent over the animal, stroked the moist coat once, and stood up. He stepped back quickly and then shut the shed door very laboriously. But in the end he had to turn round. The sky was already growing red over the forest, and he felt that the light was falling mercilessly on his face. Nor could he avoid her looking at him calmly and probingly.

"You're going for a visit?" he asked, undoing the string of his boat key unnecessarily. "He didn't guide you well—I mean, for you. He was only thinking how to get home—"

He fell silent at her smile.

"He guided us well," she answered, smiling, after a coy silence. "No it's not a real visit, it's to America we're going—"

Now he looked at her, and in his heavy, tired eyes, like those of an animal, was the startled look of a child whose toy has fallen into the water.

She looked aside, across the lake, where the first bird cries were wakening. It looked as though she were already standing aboard a ship. "Yes. We're Mormons," she added.

"Is that a religion?" he asked, downcast.

"Yes—"

When they entered the cottage, the smallholder started up out of his first sleep. "In the forest, brother," he murmured, "more to the east—"

"You can sleep first," Jürgen said. "It's not good on the water now. There's still mist. I'll take you there later on."

They both accepted gratefully, and Jürgen shook down a bed for Grotjohann by the hearth. He was already asleep when Jürgen turned round once more to see that nothing was forgotten."

"And you?" the girl asked.

"Oh—I've plenty of room in there— and I don't sleep much. Cover yourself up well and rest your feet."

"Do you live all alone?" she asked, taking off her kerchief.

"Yes—but it doesn't matter— in the forest they live alone, too."

Then he went out, softly.

On the water there was a red shimmer by now, and the divers were giving their clear, penetrating call, up river on the lake. It was going to be a hot day, and the hay could be brought in. 'America—' he thought, 'that's over the edge of the world.' He went once more to the shed, laid his hand on the animal's coat which was now dry and warm, and then slept for two hours in the tool-shed. When he pulled the blanket up, he felt a wood shaving between his fingers. 'She wasn't there,' he thought as he fell asleep, 'by the hearth—and now he's asleep there, the Mormon—perhaps it will be all right now—'

She was fetching water from the well when he returned with the nets, and she came down to the ferry to wait for him. Everything was bright about her, and when she shaded her eyes with her hand because the water was flashing in the sunlight, it was a free and lovely movement, immaculate in the face of the wide landscape. She put her hand to the chain to make the boat fast, and in this gesture too lay a familiarity with all things which was at home everywhere in the realm of human order.

"I wanted to make coffee for you," she said, "and now

I suppose you've been on the water half the night already. Was it a good catch?"

"Yes, thank you," he answered, "it's a good time now. I suppose you couldn't find the mill," he added, as he stepped out of the boat, "and—I've got only roasted barley—"

"You need a button sewn on there," she said, smiling past his embarrassment. "It isn't right that nobody looks after you."

"She died in the spring," he answered, "I thought you might have heard tell of it in your village, perhaps."

She shook her head. "That's why he said that—"

"What did he say?"

"That you—oh, never mind, he was drunk; but still, you have different eyes, that see through everything—but I'm not frightened—it's lovely here by the water, and we only had woods round the village, and the owls hooted at night—"

He looked round once, as though the landscape had become new through her praise; and since he did not know what to answer, he stepped back to the boat and began to pull out the heavy fish box, on which one of the boards was rotting. No, she was not to help, he said, it was much too heavy. There was nothing for him to do but to go into the water up to his waist and lift the box over the edge of the boat, onto his shoulders. He staggered a little on the marshy bottom, but then he climbed up slowly to the shed. The water streamed out of the holes in the box, and the greenish wood shone in the sunlight. To the girl it looked as though a strong animal had gone down to the river in the night and were now returning with vast prey, into the quiet, dewy forest. "So he was right," she said, when he stood breathing heavily beside the load he had set down. "You can lift a boat all by yourself, on your shoulders."

"He always has plenty of big talk," he protested in embarrassment, "especially when he's been drinking—but I dare say I could carry you over the river—if you were as tired as yesterday."

"Right to America," she said, and the soft laugh sounded again from deep in her throat.

It was a long time before Jürgen plucked up courage, and the smallholder was already carrying his bundle down to the boat, when he asked, with an utterly unsuccessful attempt at indifference, if she did not know of someone who would come to work for him—perhaps from her village—what she said about the button had made him think of it again— Yes, she thought she knew of someone. It sounded very thoughtful. And would this someone be content with just a little? For she could see for herself that he did not sleep on gold pieces, and as for talking, he was not much of a hand at that, either—except perhaps when people came to be ferried over, then there might be a bit of a chat— Yes, the one she meant was quite able to be content alone, and besides, there was the goat— Yes, and could he go there some time and ask the girl? No, he could save himself the journey, for the girl was here and did not fancy going to the cousin in the forest, because he had a miserly wife and because she wanted to work and earn a bit before she went out there to the foreign country.

To that he said nothing and only looked at her without comprehension, as though God had sent an angel and the angel were telling him that from now on he would dwell with him, the ferryman, Jürgen Doskocil. And she laughed a while at the look on his face, but in a way that did not hurt him.

"Yes, brother," the smallholder said, his weasel's eyes sliding, from left and right of the crooked nose, over household stuff and nets and chattels. "You are still one of those who live in error and have not yet seen the Light, but it looks as if you were decent and industrious. But it must be good pay, and two bushels of potatoes you must allot her, and a warm dress at Christmas; and it might be better if I put it in writing and came over from the forest some time, and there's much to think of, for she has been called to grace, and it's hard for me to go to the forest village alone, and you shouldn't charge me any fare money for taking me over, because it is, so to speak, an act of grace that the Lord of Hosts has entered your house so visibly—"

"It's time for you to go, father," the girl said abruptly.

Jürgen was incapable of speaking. He only nodded to everything. He nodded all during the journey and stared through half-closed eyes at the reflection of the bald head floating spectrally on the dark water beside the boat. 'A bad case, this father,' he thought after an hour. 'He's talked more in this hour than I have in my whole life. His head's like a beehive. But there will be a fire in the hearth when I come home – perhaps America will sink into the sea by then – they say there are big earthquakes over there – '

Up to dark he was busy at the ferry, for it was market day and the carts did not return to the moor village until late. She was sitting on the doorstep when he came walking up from the last crossing.

"It sounds nice," she said, "when they hit the iron over there and shout *Fetch over*."

"Yes," he answered, "but sometimes they make a fool of me. Then it's the children from over there. And they sing, too – but you mustn't mind that."

A heron flapped low and heavily along the river, and its hoarse call broke manifold against the walls of the night. The mist was rising, pushing slowly between them and the world.

"Is it true," she asked softly, "that you can talk with the dead?"

He snuffed out the lantern, looking into the light for a while before he did it.

"I sometimes see – " he answered humbly, "a second body – behind the first body – but now it won't come again, for now you are the blessing at my fireside – "

For a while the words still hung, echoing and alight in the motionless air, and each of them heard the other's breath, timidly avoiding the image so that it might not fade out.

"Good night," she then said quietly and went into the house.

»» *Chapter Three* ««

SUMMER PASSED OVER THE EARTH WITH many thunderstorms and in the thundery weather the fish rose and filled the nets. It was a good year for the catch. And when Jürgen came home, he went through house and yard until he had found Marte.

"You brought luck," he said.

She raised her eyes from her work and smiled. "Don't put the luck on my shoulders," she answered, "for if it falls off some time, it will be my fault, and that won't do."

It took a while before he grasped that; he could never understand how anyone could so easily say things that had to be untangled first, like a net in which a pike had been struggling half the night. "It doesn't seem to look for the broad shoulders," he said as he turned to go out, "else it could easily have stayed with me—"

In this summer Jürgen began to make plans. Before there had been nothing in his life but the boat and the nets, the ferry and his little domain with the goat as its center. So it would remain, and only if he were to lift a lump of gold out of the lake would it be possible to move the walls out a bit further, so that perhaps a cow might be included within the limits of his existence, or even—but it was presumptuous to think of a horse.

But something like a solid wall had grown underneath his feet, carrying him higher from day to day, a base on which to brace oneself for lifting a heavy burden onto the shoulders with a light heart. For now the house was clean and neat, and watercress grew at the windows, and in the evening light when he came into the room the calm flames burnt in the hearth, and no shadow sat there, cold and transparent.

And so, when the young rollers were beginning to flock in the alders by the water, Jürgen Doskocil signed the lease with the forest administration and, coming back towards evening, he walked round the piece of ground that was now his. It was a waste clearing at the edge of the old timber forest, covered by a few gray-green drift-blocks, the charred stumps of some pines that had once stood high, and a wilderness of willow herb, its red flowers rocking in the breeze like a tiny forest. He knelt down by one of the stones, pushed the crushed pale grass and lichen aside and lifted the dark cool soil from the depths to the light. It lay heavy in his hands, like bread. 'There'll be oats,' he thought, 'golden ears as it might be from the caverns of the folk down below—bread for horses first—and then—then perhaps some day bread for men.'

He let his hand rest in the cool hollow, and he remembered the night when he had kneeled before the grave and sacrificed ring and kerchief for the dead woman. "Jesus Christ help you with His Blood," he said silently to the earth. And the discontented lines in the dead woman's face, which had risen before his eyes, changed into a delicate network of roots from which the oats would grow here; and however slowly and heavily his thoughts might move, he felt as though the earth's blood and the blood from his heart were transfusing through his hand and in this way death were changing into life.

He came again with Marte, when sunset over the moor was casting its reddish glow onto his new ground. He walked round the clearing with her and then he pointed once to the dark soil, on which the dew already lay. "Bread," he said. "Our daily bread—"

Not until they were walking back did he tell her all about it, from beginning to end.

"And all by yourself?" she asked anxiously. "With your hands?"

He smiled. "With the shoulders," he answered. "The small ones for luck and the broad ones for bread."

From this evening on, the waste clearing came to secret life every day after sunset. On the drift block in the middle, which Jürgen had resolved to let lie, 'because the forest folk down below live beneath it,' the hunchback would sit, his long arms folded round his knees that were drawn up under his chin, and watch how in the pale, white light of the summer nights the fisherman's gigantic figure attacked the stones or the deep-growing pine roots. His shadow, broad and foreshortened, was like the shadow of a bear, and there was no other sound of his work but the heavy breathing from his chest and now and then the clear ring of the crowbar striking on a stone, or the squeak of a root being pulled from the earth.

In the beginning, the hunchback would stare into the dusk with aching eyes, helpless before this picture of strength that was tearing open the earth before him, and so much was he a witness of this great work that his own weak arms ached at each movement of Jürgen's hands when they lifted a stone or loosened a tree stump. But then the soul behind his somber eyes would begin to fill irresistibly with all that was outside him; the black outlines of the treetops and the red glow behind them, the gleam of the moon, its silent crescent rising over the forest, the sad cry of the birds calling to their own kind high over the water, and the bitter scent of the alders and the rushes, whose leaves were opening to breathe in the night dew.

Then he stretched out his hand for the flute of birch bark, raised it to his lips and began to draw from it one of those slowly falling tunes with which he often woke an echo over his flock in the hills, so that it might assure him of his being and bring him that response which man denied him. Now it sounded like a bird in the darkening branches, now it was like the lament of a child in a lonely house, and sometimes it was nothing more than the wandering of the wind over reeds and grasses and the falling of raindrops in the veiled woods. But it was as remote from anger as from pain, and was like solitary talking on the brink of sleep, and it did not rise as something adrift through the moonlight, but might have been the sound of the stone on which he sat, ancient and very holy, and no animal in the forest would have halted in fright at his song.

Then Jürgen stood in the hollow which he had dug in the ground, leaning on his crowbar, and to him it was as though these strains were the dark fallow earth which he was breaking open, speaking to him with a primal chaotic voice, as the water spoke to him, and the wind. For life, to him, did not end with the breathing human face, and not only the dead rose before his heavy eyes. There were also the faces of the stones and of the animals, and a gentle twilight cloaked all creation for him, because only the uncreated was without life.

Once, after their work was done, when they were sitting on the stone that was like the seat of some ancient gods, they saw a dark animal standing silently at the edge of the clearing. The cripple's hand gripped Jürgen's arm, and they both felt a cool breeze rising among the leaves, moving over their faces, and dying away behind them. A cloud passed slowly over the moon, burying and suffocating her, extinguishing the bluish, comforting light. And after that the edge of the clearing was as before and the leaves hung motionless in the gleaming light.

"A wolf? Was it a wolf?" Heini whispered.

But Jürgen shook his head. "They feel me digging," he said. "The ground trembles under their feet and so they come to see what is happening here."

Yet a faint spell still hung over the field that was coming into being, and Jürgen lifted out the roots as carefully as if he were lifting a sheet from a sleeping face.

She was sitting at the hearth and spinning, when he came home; and even before he opened the door he heard the quiet singing sound of the wheel, vibrating through the wood of the beams. His first glance went into the twilight at the back of the hearth, and only then it came to rest in the light of the lamp.

"No one has been here," she said quietly. "Sit down and rest now."

He sat mending his nets, feeling the peace of her eyes for a while before the darkness of his room surrounded him.

"Soon the wild geese will be going," he said from behind the smoke clouds of his pipe. "You know where they go to?"

No, she didn't know. Of course, the teacher had said that they flew to Africa, but he always pretended to know something about everything and she didn't trust him. She thought that such gray birds wouldn't look right on the Nile—it was on the Nile that the little basket had floated with the child Moses in it, and what would the gray, sad birds be doing on such waters?

"Perhaps they—perhaps they fly right to America?" he suggested in a low voice.

"America is far away," she answered and looked past him at the little window, beyond which the night lay dark and silent.

"Yes, it must be a long way—" he said, gazing into the black opening of the hearth.

Sometimes it happened that even at this late hour the droning clang of the plowshare came from the other side of the river. For more people were traveling than was usual at the end of summer, strangers who asked the way and spoke of hunger and of its satisfaction; and there were those who, as they put the coin in Jürgen's hand and turned away, said that the world must change and must become just and equal and without slavery. This was nothing to which Jürgen knew an answer; but sometimes then he would stand for a while, leaning on his pole, and watch the stranger vanish into the shadow of the oaks.

And every time Marte was standing on the doorstep, looking his way with uneasy eyes.

"Are you waiting?" he asked once.

"No, but I'm afraid. It's uncanny when it calls like that from over there. There's so much that might be wandering through the night."

"Water and men are always on their way," he answered. "Don't be afraid, my hands are strong."

"It isn't the hands," she said absently.

'She belongs to someone,' Jürgen thought. 'She is sure to belong to someone, and one day the plowshare will sound—*Fetch over!* And that will be him. A townsman, probably, with a stiff collar and gloves. "Miss Grotjohann here? Good. And you're the master, I suppose? H'm. Yes, she's going to be my wife, you know. I hope she's been comfortable here, in this fisherman's cabin." And then the other will sit by his hearth and she will make him coffee, and *he*, oh yes, he would probably go and look after the goat or at his new field or see to the nets. An old boat—when the new one comes it is pushed aside. Then water comes up through the broken joints, moss creeps over it—finished—done with—'

In September the work in the clearing was so far advanced that he could start plowing. He did not want to use horses, but the stones which lay deep in the ground knocked the plowshare from Heini's hands. So he borrowed two horses from the parson, and in the evening the upturned soil lay there black and shining. He brought the team back and once more, on his way home, he went to his field. Rain was drizzling from low-hanging clouds, and he lifted a handful of earth to his face. It smelt of sleep and of the depths, and when he had crumbled it between his hands the smell remained with him and went with him, as if taking root in his body.

When he came up from the water, where he had been to fetch a forgotten net, in the red shaft of light falling from the window he saw a dark figure. From below it looked as if a tree stood there, but Jürgen knew that there was no tree there and he saw the tense attitude of a lurker watching his quarry.

At first it seemed to him to be someone frozen into the gray ice; but then he recognized the village inn keeper's son, of whose love affairs many stories were told. 'Ah, my friend,' he thought almost gratefully, 'now that isn't a good way for you to be going.' There was only the wet grass pressed down under his bare feet, and so the grip of his hand came as if it had grown right out of the air.

"Forgotten something?" he asked softly.

For a moment the body in front of him seemed to double up. Then it covered its face with both hands and with a sudden jump tried to escape into the darkness. But Jürgen's hand did not loosen its grip.

"You need to hang in the river," he said, "to cool you off a bit. Or have a ring through your nose like the bull on the estate. Next time, my lad, you won't have a bone left unbroken in your body, understand?" And he kicked him so that he tumbled out of the shaft of light as if falling into a void. Behind the fleeing feet, silence closed in again, and not till a while later did a familiar whistle on two fingers sound from the direction of the village. Jürgen stared into the dark, which seemed to have split open, and from there to the red window glowing defenselessly in the huge night. 'But one day it will be the right one,' he thought before he entered the house.

After supper he asked her whether she had made any friends in the village. She looked at him in surprise. No, she had no friends. She would go shopping, have a chat with the inn keeper, and then come back.

"Be careful," he said after a while, when he had begun to work on a new net. "Lock the house when I'm on the water, for they're like bulls here."

She didn't reply, but later when he looked at her from

under the shadow of his brows, he saw that she had blushed up to the roots of her hair.

He was hit by the change in her face, as if by the heavy push of a wave, and it washed away from him the somber coverings of his reserve. He trembled, and this trembling spread till it reached his heavy hands working at the meshes of the net. He saw the crown of her lowered head and saw that she was like a saint amidst the poverty of his house and his life. 'I should stroke her,' he thought, 'like stroking a child's head—but she would only think that I as well—I said a bad word—that about the bulls—'

He stood up hastily and hung the net on the wooden peg in the timbered wall. The rain was beating on the window.

"That's good for the field," he said. "The grain will lie as warm as with a mother."

"Yes," she said, without looking up.

He went to the front of the house again, stood in the dark of the small yard and listened. The rain fell in his hair and put up a rustling wall around his face. The last light went out in the village. He thought he heard footsteps, something creeping round the cottage, holding its breath, but it was his blood streaming to his heart. Nobody was there, only the soft sound of the ground drinking the rain. It was a sound like that the drinking child had made, the child which had not been his own and which had been under the ground for so long a time now. And the drops must be running over the little coffin, slowly and as dark as in in his veins. How beautiful it must be to have a child, something helpless to put one's hands round.

He only woke again when the raindrops trickled out of his hair and down his cheeks; then he circled the house again, made a secret sign in all four quarters of the wind, and went to his room. Before he lay down he locked the door and hung the key up under the old engraving of Saint Peter casting his nets, which his grandfather had once come by.

From this night on the rain remained over the land. Mist hung on the woods and the earth overflowed, so that the dark river no longer seemed an abyss but like a bridge. The summer corn rotted, and on the fields for the winter lay black water; the potatoes began to molder before they could be stored in the cellars. From the drowning tenements of the earth the beasts rose up and fled into the barns of man, where they destroyed the scanty stores of food.

At first people stood at their doors, looking at the clouds, waiting. Then they could be seen at midday standing in the fields, putting their hands into a sheaf, pulling a dripping wet potato plant out of the ground. And then the villages remained silent, dark, dead. The crows gathered in the withering trees over the farms, a dog strayed through the fields digging the last mice out of their holes. It was as if the rain were bitter and poisonous. Not only did moss grow on the wet roofs, not only were the plows and harrows which still stood waiting in the fields covered with rust; the very souls of men were eaten and slowly destroyed by the breath of approaching fate. Sheaves disappeared from the fields, potato fields were emptied overnight by unknown hands. The locks of barns were opened by force, and in the early hours of evening now and then the clamor of a quarrel rose, the hatred of a broil flared up from the darkened village, accompanied by the wailing of the womenfolk and the barking of dogs.

Only the fish went their way now as before, and twice a week Jürgen went to town in the big boat. Once more he stood in the shop and bargained for a bright kerchief, but when he sat by the hearth again, holding his hands out to the flames, he did not dare go to his room and come back with the rustling tissue paper. 'She might think I want to bribe her to stay,' he thought; and so he only unpacked the things he had bought for housekeeping.

Then they sat by the fire, Marte with her sewing and Jürgen with his nets. The rain formed a singing wall round the house. "The oats," Jürgen said sometimes, lifting his head to listen. "If we can't sow in time—"

"The Golden City grew in the wilderness," she answered quietly. "The oats will grow, too, if it is His Will."

Then he went on knotting the meshes in the torn net, but his eyes saw through them into the flames in the hearth. Walls and towers grew there, glaring with gold, bridges rose high and crumbled again behind the fleeting footsteps. Palaces flared up under the glow of sparks, archways collapsed, and temples ascended. And over all that there was a strange, far, lamenting sound, the sound of another world into which a human face went and vanished out of sight.

At the end of October, Jürgen sowed the oats. For two days a cold wind blew over the glimmering field, and out of the gray houses the people came forth, reluctant and distrustful. Jürgen's field was like a well which drank the water, and on the second day, about noon, he could load the oats onto his little cart and tie on the seed apron. Then he went back once more, because he had forgotten a piece of cord, and he stopped on the threshold. Marte was kneeling on the floorboards by the hearth, her forehead resting on her clasped hands. It shocked him so, that against his will he uttered an inarticulate sound. But she only lifted her calm face to him and said softly; "This is our way, we pray whenever something goes into the earth, a human being or a grain of corn."

"Yes," he said without thinking and closed the door again silently.

Outside he stood, confused, beside his cart. He put the harness round his shoulders but forgot about going to the field. 'She's different,' he thought, 'a face from the Golden City—God could live with her, but not someone like me—and surely I am like an animal in her eyes.'

Then he pulled the load through the heavy earth, up to his field. There were patches of blue in the windswept sky, but his heart was heavy. When he had tied on his sowing apron and plunged his hand into the cool oats, for an instant he was tempted to kneel down like the girl; but he was ashamed, as of a lie, and his thoughts went down stealthily to the folk below, and there they asked help for the young seed.

And then he walked along the furrows, throwing the grain into the black soil. Cranes sailed away high above him, and the great forest roared in the strong wind. But he did not look up. Before his hands he saw the girl's face, remote, strange, and glorified, and with every step he felt how a dark root went deeper and deeper down into his heart, splitting its strength and filling it slowly with a bitter taste, up to the rim.

He hid that from himself, but in the early twilight, when he was pulling the harrow along, he knew that there the heavy thing was again, which dwelt in him and made his other eyes open to see a sight that was not there. Suddenly he shook himself like an animal starting up out of some lair. He stopped, lifted his head, and turned his gaze into the shadow of the forest. But there was nothing to be seen, only swaying branches, somber trunks, and a torn sky with gaps from which a yellow light fell, cold and evil. He looked out for a while, then shook his heavy head and walked on quietly until his work was done; and as he walked, he saw at every turning the red glow from the window of his cottage grow more and more comforting in the gathering darkness.

When he pulled the cart into the shed, the first drops of rain were falling, and he stopped for a moment at the door and with tired eyes saw the rain falling on the corn; and he thought that it had been good to sow before the new flood. There was nobody sitting at the back of the hearth.

"It's growing," he said, as he stepped into the lamplight.

Darkness filled his room and he sat upright in his bed and peered into the bodiless dark. His limbs ached, but again and again he opened his heavy lids. The rain was rustling on the low roof and every drop that fell into the waterbutt measured the passing of time with a clear, mechanical ring. It sounded like a clock whose hand moved calmly but inexorably on. Someone was coming. Jürgen did not see him, but he felt how somewhere the night divided, the rain split open, and then the rustling closed in again behind something. So he was not startled by the droning clang of the plowshare. The old clock in the room took up the sound, vibrating long after it had died away. Silently and hastily he dressed, slipped on his oilskins, and took keys, pole and lantern.

There was Marte standing at the door. Her face was white. The lamp was lit over the hearth. "It called," she whispered.

"For the market," he answered. "What are you frightened of? It isn't for the first time."

But she looked right through him towards the other bank, and then the sound came across the water again, and Jürgen went out.

His name was Maclean and for a year he had been the preacher for all the Mormons in that part of the country.

He had been standing beside the plowshare on the other side of the river, wrapped in a dark cloak, waiting until the ferry struck the bank. Did Sister Marte Grotjohann live in the ferry house, he had asked in his harsh impeccable German. He was her priest, he said. Jürgen had not even lifted the lantern to flash it into the stranger's face. "Yes," he had answered in a low voice and ferried him over without speaking.

Then he had knocked at Marte's door. "Your priest's come."

And then he had gone into the shed and shaken himself down a bed beside the workbench.

Half an hour later the latch was pressed down. "Why do you sleep here, Jürgen?" Marte asked.

"He'd better sleep in my room. A priest can't lie in a shed."

There was a long pause, during which he heard the pouring of the rain beyond the open door. Her feet rustled in the dry wood shavings, and then he felt her quick breathing over his face. He lay like a dead tree.

"I'm frightened, Jürgen – "

"Why?"

"He's like the angel with the flaming sword – I kneel, but he'll drive me out."

"Do you believe in his God?"

"Yes."

"And where will he drive you out from?"

"From here."

With his left hand he lifted the blanket from his bed and spread it round her shivering body, too. There was a smell of freshly cut wood. The mice rustled in the shavings, and the rain poured down over the dark world.

"It's poor living with me," he said at last, "and hard bread – the Golden City is far away and my back is bent

— sometimes I see the dead with my eyes, and I don't know how to talk, in the evening, by the fire — but if you don't want to, no one shall drive you out. Not even a lamb can be driven, if it doesn't want to. You can take it on your shoulders and carry it away, but you can't drive it."

She drew one deep breath, like a child that has stopped crying, and the warmth of her blood, now growing calmer, filled the narrow space under the rough blanket which enfolded both of them. Jürgen knew nothing of all the old tales of love, in which a naked sword lay between man and woman. But he knew that she had come to him in fear and perplexity, defenseless, no more than an unprotected child. In his heavy thoughts the man loomed up whom he had just fetched over and whose distant shadow had darkened the whole day for him; and the field loomed up on which he had sown the oats, and the girl whose breathing he could feel on his shoulder. And out of all this rose — he would not have been able to say how — a feeling of humble happiness, an image of the field, the hearth and quiet sunsets, something that would grow, that must be guarded under hollowed hands, like a young plant against the cold wind.

"No one will drive you out," he said once more. "But go now, else he may think evil of you."

"Yes," she answered humbly. "Good night."

He heard her feet among the shavings, the pouring of the rain grew louder through the open door, and then everything was again as it had been before a running stream of darkness, silence and time.

He pressed his face into the warmth still lingering where she had been, and for a moment it sounded as if he groaned with the pain of a wound.

Rain was still falling the next day. Mist hung over the forest in a monotonous gray sky without a rift, without the shapes of clouds. Jürgen was on the water for a long time. He saw that someone had tried to force the lock on one of the fish boxes and he realized that he would have to remove the boxes overnight, preferably upstream above the ferry, where nobody would expect to find them. He sat idle in the boat a while longer, his hands clasped, and gazed over towards the two villages, which lay like two big grave mounds in the mist. 'A hard winter,' he thought. 'If the ice holds, they'll begin to steal, and then they'll be murdering each other—' And he reckoned up what was still needed before the snow came; flour, firewood, bacon, paraffin, fodder for the goat, the dress for Marte—the priest, yes, that must be settled today.

When he entered the room, Maclean was sitting by the hearth. There was a coffee cup beside him, and in his hands he held a book that looked like a small Bible. At first Jürgen saw merely these things. The night before he had seen only a dark figure and had avoided looking into the face; and even now he only saw the hands, white, narrow, very long hands, with broad, flat nails that suggested furtive digging. It seemed to him as though there were two separate beings sitting there, one consisting of these two hands, quite alone, and dangerous as two fiendish beasts; and one that had its existence only behind them. And it was to this second being that he now raised his eyes and said: "Good day."

The face did not alter at his greeting. It was narrow and angular, with dark, straight hair and eyes set close together. Jürgen had not seen many faces in his life, and those he had seen, good and bad, had been somehow alike in the dullness and limitation of their outlines. They were alike, as fish were alike, no matter whether pike or tench. But this was a face of quite another kind, and Jürgen knew that it would feel cold if he were to touch it.

"Good day," Maclean said, and it seemed as if he did not have to open his lips in order to speak. "So you are the fisherman?"

"Yes," Jürgen answered, "I'm the fisherman."

He was still standing at the door, which he had shut after him, holding an oar before him in both hands, in his gray fisherman's coat that reached down to his knees, his gaze under the heavy brows fixed on the slight, black figure which was like that of a boy. It was the searching, rather melancholy gaze of a man for whom every change, whether in the water, in the sky or in his house, meant anxiety which his eyes must read and probe to its very roots.

The stranger answered this look, and while his gray eyes mustered the fisherman from his feet up to his disheveled shock of hair, a thin smile flickered over his mouth, as rapidly as a flash from a turning mirror. And in the instant of this flicker, Jürgen knew that it might perhaps become necessary to break this man's neck, and he felt it queer that this thought did not horrify him at all. He shook his head imperceptibly, put the oar down by the hearth, and pulled the wet coat from his shoulders.

"When will the gentleman be moving on?" he asked quietly.

Maclean lifted the hand with the Bible slightly, as though to ward off an objection, and then let it drop again. "The word of the Prophet," he answered sternly, "must remain with those who await it."

"Maybe those who wait for it are a long way off," Jürgen suggested.

"Sin is always close at hand."

"I should be pleased to show the gentleman the way," Jürgen said, taking an ember from the fire and putting it on the tobacco in his pipe.

The white face became still narrower. "It seems to me," he said, "that this daughter of our Church has need of me."

Jürgen was already standing at the door. "It is the custom in these parts, the gentleman should understand, that each man can go to his church, but it is not the custom with us for the church to come to every man. I have a small house, and the church is too big for it. Where has the gentleman his coat?"

"You will repent of it," Maclean said and stood up.

Jürgen opened the door and stepped outside. "Yonder is the next village," he said, pointing into the damp mist. "The road leads there. They drink a lot and they'll soon be starving. But there perhaps the gentleman can collect a congregation."

"Peter was a fisherman," Maclean said, pulling his dark cloak more tightly round him, "but not all fishermen are fishers of men as he was—"

Jürgen only smiled into the malevolent foreign face, but his smile faded out as the dark figure disappeared in the mist. And before he went into the house, he turned suddenly as though it might step out again from some spot in the white wall.

That autumn the fields around the two villages remained without winter sowing. It rained until well into November. Then the wind veered to the east, and the next morning the ice was glittering over the fields. And after another two weeks it began to snow, without any wind, and snowed for three days and three nights. And after that there was a muffled, shrouded land. River and lake were frozen over, and for three days Jürgen was out and about from dawn to sunset, breaking holes in the ice so that the fish should not suffocate. Then he sharpened ax and saw and started work in the big timber clearings of the forest. "The animals will come into people's houses," he said, "and after the animals will come the people who have no bread left. We must see that we give them more than a passage from the Bible."

Then he sat in the darkness by the hearth and ate the soup that Marte had cooked. Only the fire gave light to the room, and when he looked to his side he saw the girl's shadowy head in the pillows, looking at him in silence.

"It's not right to stay in the warm," she said, "when you've got to go out, and to go to sleep again when around you there's nothing but the dark trees."

But he shook his head. "You're young," he answered, "and just like a little bird that has to stay warm. It's quiet all day. Go to sleep now and never mind."

The first morning, when he was ready, ax and saw over his shoulder, his fur cap pulled down over his forehead, he nodded to her, and she stretched out her hand to him from under the bedclothes. He stepped to her bed and carefully took the hand she held out to him. He saw her arm up to the shoulder, white and fragile, as it seemed to him, and his day's work seemed easy after so much beauty. He said nothing, only once his horny fingers stroked over her wrist, where the veins showed blue under the thin skin. And so it was every morning from now on.

It was night when Jürgen went to the forest, and it was night when he returned home. A small track made by his footsteps ran straight as the furrow of a plow across the forest to his working site, an hour and a half's walk, and left and right of it lay the immaculate snow, the tree trunks, and the silence. Only at the edge of the forest the path twisted a little to one side and led to the edge of the snow covered field. Animals' tracks ran across the white surface, and here and there they had scraped away the snow with their hooves, to get at the corn. Here Jürgen stood every evening, looking across the field, listening to the frost tinkling in the trunks of the old forest, and he leaned forward towards the earth, as if he were listening to a child asleep.

The dead day of the week was Saturday, for the fire burnt in the hearth but Marte was not there. She was among the community of the saints. Nobody could understand how it had happened, but Maclean had founded a congregation in the village. They had given him a tumbledown cabin at the edge of the forest, and every Saturday he preached in one of the peasant's houses. "God's wrath shall arise over this land," he would say. "The earth shall be barren as the wombs of your women. Children shall be carried to the graveyard and dead cattle to the carrion pit. Wolves shall prowl round the houses, and out of the waters the evil one shall arise. But the Golden City waits afar, and God's hand rests on her towers. Corn grows out of her earth, and vineyards cover the hills. And God opens His arms to receive the faithful of all the earth who turn again to His true word." Then the women and girls wept, and the peasants and smallholders looked into the white, gaunt face and saw behind it the waves of the ocean and themselves gliding out into this new paradise, with no hunger and no want. And Marte too knelt in the darkest corner, her hands folded over her heart, and between the golden towers she saw the heavy, lonely face of Jürgen Doskocil, as he sat by the hearth warming his stiffened hands over the flames, with the silence of the roof over his bowed head.

And once, as she came back quietly and even humbler than usual, she found him at the fireside, his shoulders bent and one of her kerchiefs in his hands, as though he had wrapped it round a wound.

"That's—yes—my hands were so cold—" he said and took the kerchief back to her basket. But he made a semicircle away from the hearth, as though a guest were sitting there, and she noticed how softly he trod and that there was the look of a frightened child in his eyes. Then she know that a guest from beyond had been there and that the shadows had fallen upon him again while she had been building her Golden City.

Before Christmas, when Jürgen left the timber clearing at dusk, he saw the first wolf track crossing his path. He bent down and put his fingers into the deep imprints. Although the snow was cold, he felt as though something of the unknown animal's warmth were penetrating into his body. He looked round searchingly, but the thicket on his right was like a shuttered house, and on the left the timber forest lay in twilight and the trees stood dark, motionless, menacing. 'It might be a dog turned wild,' he thought. But then he shook his head. He remembered that Marte was in the village, and he began to run, head down like a heavy animal, and at every step the edge of the ax clinked against the blade of the saw.

He waited for her at the end of the village, still some way from Maclean's cabin. The preacher accompanied her, and the sound of their lowered voices came ahead of them. Jürgen saw only their gestures, and before he could understand a word he went to meet them.

"The wolves are in the forest," he said, "I shall wait for

you." Then he turned round and walked away from them quickly.

"Fear not the wolves of the forest," Maclean said in his high pitched carrying voice, "but fear the wolves that put on sheep's clothing—"

He walked faster, as far as the first half-buried bush, which stood out of the snow like a landmark in the sea of whiteness.

"I saw prints," was all he said, when Marte came. "Someone must be with you."

Only when they crossed the threshold did she look at him.

"When will you have a day of rest, Jürgen?" she asked.

"When your God allows," he answered after a while.

»» *Chapter Four* ««

ALWAYS AFTER MARTE HAD STRETCHED OUT her arm in the morning darkness to give Jürgen her hand, she lay like that for a while longer, her bare arm reaching out into the dark, cool room, and listened to the heavy footsteps going into the distance, the frozen snow crackling under them until they faded into the obscurity of the forest. The room was still filled with a flickering red glow from the fire, but already the dark and the silence closed in round the cottage from all sides, narrowing the circle of life, barring threshold and windows, and building behind the cottage walls and roof another wall and another roof, where she was the only living thing, with the beating of her heart, the drumming of her blood and the prickling cold on the skin of her bare arm.

She looked down at this arm that belonged to her and yet was like something strange, outside herself. She saw the gentle contours of its form, the delicacy of the joints, and the white of the skin reflecting the red glow from the fire. And in the simplicity of her thoughts an image rose, as though this living, articulated shape were waiting for something that hesitated or did not dare to come, because that other growth of wall and roof stood between her and the outer world.

Then the gathering darkness of the room began to come alive with fleeting visions, visions of the past and of the future. The blood of her body, become tranquil in hard daily work and the slow tide of her master's life, began to press back again towards her past and rinse the pictures of joy and pleasure clear of what overlay them —began to ask the emptiness whether no one wanted it. And before all the faces two rose up, the heavy and somehow mighty face of Jürgen Doskocil, and the gleaming pallid face of the foreigner, behind which burnt the magic of a sensual faith, the miracle of the Golden City, and the mercilessness of a terrible God, whose faith threw itself like a burning body upon the bodies of the faithful.

She did not analyze all this into conscious sentences. She only had the dull feeling in her blood that she was desired, alike by Jürgen Doskocil's earth and Maclean's heaven. She thought of the few minutes when she had lain by Jürgen's side, untouched by his hands but in the glow of his heavy blood; and out of the memories of her past she went, drawn and driven, further along the path of her dream images, up to the point where they broke in sheer bliss. And in all the unknown tangle of her soul, she felt unmistakably that she was drowning in the bliss of weakness when Jürgen's image led her to the end—and that she was shattered in the bliss of terror when she thought of the emissary of God. It seemed as though she were committing sin with God, and that it would not be possible to go on living after such wild ecstasy.

When she had come so far, she drew her arm back hastily, frightened as if one of the two were reaching out for her, and pressed it against the warmth of her body, as though coming to herself again. But the short sleep till daylight was heavy and tense, as though she were listening for footsteps approaching the house, which would liberate her with decisive action from the unrest in her blood. But even in dream she did not know which tread she should be waiting for, and both faces merged, floated clear of each other and drew together again, until they drowned in the well of sleep.

For many days, after Jürgen had waited for her at the end of the village, she thought of his humble and melancholy words: "When your God allows—" And her feet went their way in her day's work as though wrapped in long veils. For she knew nothing of God. The God of the Golden City was far away, still further away than the God of her pastor who had confirmed her. Maclean was there in His place, the visible and audible, and what he gave of bread and promise, of menace and punishment, he gave into her hand out of the hand of God. 'When Maclean gives it—' she thought and knelt in the darkest corner of the congregation, her forehead bowed down to the floor, and left the room hastily after the hour of prayer, so that he should not approach her and press her hard with his burning eyes.

But one evening, after Christmas, he caught up with her. It was snowing out of murky, still air, and she did not hear him until he had stretched out his hand for her arm.

"You are avoiding me," he said in a low voice. "Are you in sin, sister?"

She saw a pale shimmer instead of his face, like that from the rotting wood she kept behind the stove, which gleamed in the darkness. "No," she whispered. But she had to stop, because the question caught at her breath and did not let go.

His hand was still fastened on her arm, so hard that it hurt, and the other hand was suddenly laid upon her right breast. "He has commanded," he said in the same low voice, "that no man shall know a virgin until God has known her—through—through—his priest. Do you understand?"

She bent her head, and only from the trembling of her body under his hands could he feel that she had understood. Holding her like that, without changing the position of his hands, he led her away from the road, towards the cabin where he lived. But at the moment when she put her foot on the narrow step, she turned her set face and looked past him, over his shoulder, over the whiteclad fields. Out of the motionless air, in which all sound carried a long way, a muffled sound penetrated the rigidity of her blood, like the noise of a door being slammed, when the hinges complained before the wood struck hard and clear against the doorpost. It sounded like the cottage door when it was slammed hastily; she had asked Jürgen to oil it that morning.

And before Maclean became aware of the resistance in her steps, they both started at the heavy, droning clangor over the fields, once, and once again, like cold metal touching them, grazing them and leaving them behind, the voice of the plowshare by Jürgen's ferry.

She had torn herself from his hands before he could recognize the sound. The darkness swallowed her up. When he rushed after her it was too late. For a third time, quieter now, like a soothing echo, this clangor came over the fields, and it was like an impenetrable wall in front of his face so that he stopped short with a curse, his body leaning forward as though in search of an opening.

Then he returned slowly to his cabin, lit the lamp and looked round the bare room with a rancorous smile. A hard mattress on a camp bed, a hearth where the fire had died, a table with a Bible and a crucifix on it, a chair, a picture of the Golden City hanging on the white-washed wall—that was all. A somber harshness filled the room, unrelenting, and it did not give way even when he began, with stiff fingers, to make a fire in the hearth. He remained sitting before the crackling flames, his hands with broad-tipped fingers folded, and stared into the feeble glow. Then he bent down, lifted the fender around the hearth, and took something from beneath it. This was wrapped in greaseproof paper and looked like a bundle of letters. He unfolded the paper and arranged the cards in his hand. They were photographs of naked girls, kneeling, their gaze upturned to the beholder; and on every face was the same expression, an equal mixture of shame, fear and penitent abandon. He held the cards like a pack of playing cards, lowered them between his knees so that the light of the fire fell on them, and sat there like a tired beast of prey toying with a paralyzed quarry.

When the snow outside the cabin creaked faintly, he lifted his head, listening, and nodded as though he already knew from the sound of the footsteps who it was. He pushed the packet back under the fender and opened the door only after the knocking had been repeated, insistently, several times.

It was a peasant girl, who looked round the room with restless eyes.

"Confession?"

"Yes."

"Undress. God wishes to bless you."

»» ««

Jürgen Doskocil was still standing beside the plowshare, when Marte appeared out of the white dusk of the fields. They went into the house together without speaking. She took off her jacket, untied her kerchief and hung both on the nail beside her bed. After she had looked round the room once, as if she had returned home after a journey, she took the Bible from her chair by the hearth and laid it on the shelf at the head of her bed. Then she put some more wood on the fire.

"How did you know?" she asked, without turning her face.

The knife, with which he was working at a new oar, did not pause.

"I didn't know anything," he answered. "But things here were suddenly restless. You know what I mean? They didn't move, and nothing fell off the wall, but they were restless. Like animals before a thunderstorm. And so I went there – was there anything – anything to know?"

"Yes," she said in a low voice, "and it was good that you called."

Late in the evening, when Jürgen wound the clock, carefully letting the thin chain with its heavy weights slip through his hard hands, he suddenly paused and listened. A muffled bumping sounded from the workshed or the goatshed, as of a body throwing itself against a wooden wall and of a chain rubbing against an iron ring.

"Grita!" Marte cried, startled.

Grita was the goat. They found it with moist, heaving flanks, pressed back into a corner of the shed, as far as the chain would allow. When Jürgen lit the lantern, it pressed itself, trembling, against the human bodies and began to moan quietly. They looked around the shed, but the low walls were undamaged and there was nothing unusual to be seen.

"Let's look outside," Jürgen said. And there, when

they walked around the shed with the lantern, they saw the deep paw marks and the place where the snow had been scratched away from under the door.

"The wolf," Jürgen said.

It was still snowing, and in the red glow cast on the snow by the lantern the white flakes fell abruptly out of the dark, one after the other, as though they would never stop, soundlessly and inexorably drifting to earth, as if to bury it. And just as silently and inexorably the dark, straight, inevitable spoor ran through the circle of light, appearing out of the dark and passing out into the dark.

They both stood bent down to the ground, staring at the sinister signs. There was ill omen in the dark track, as ill omen stands at the dark entrance of a cavern.

"The otter stake," Jürgen murmured, "I'll set the otter stake—for the devil." The poor man's hatred of the beast of prey deepened his voice, and when he stood up straight and peered into the night, where the buried forest lay invisible, his right hand opened, and Marte saw that it would be capable of throttling a living creature.

"Evil things are about," she whispered. "Come inside."

Jürgen fetched the otter trap from the shed, oiled the rusted joints before the hearth, tied the fine string, and began cautiously to adjust it. It had two straight prongs, each a fathom long, with sharp spikes as long as a finger. He pressed them apart carefully until the string was taut, and pushed the safety catch back warily with a long beech log. The trap lay on the floor boards like a centipede. Then, leaning well back, he touched the string, and with a grinding noise the trap jumped into the air like a living thing, striking its jagged arms together with a clatter.

"In the old days," he said, looking down at the trap, "they say the fishermen caught people in it who stole their nets at night—my grandfather told me about it when I was small. They set it in the water, and whoever got caught was drowned—"

"Are you going to set it?" she asked after a while.

"Yes—for the wolf."

When Jürgen had put out the candle in his room and was waiting for sleep, Marte came barefooted to his bed. "It's time, Jürgen," she whispered against his shoulder. "I can't wait any more."

It was a long time before he was able to speak. Then he lifted her up in his arms and carried her back to her bed. "It's too cold for you in my room," he said softly.

She pressed herself against his chest. "But you won't go away, Jürgen?"

"I'll never go away now," he answered.

It did not escape Maclean's notice that Marte had ceased to be afraid. She knelt in the corner of the meeting room as usual, and she was as humble as ever when he spoke to her on her way home. But her humility passed through him, as if through an impersonal mediator, to God. He had become a priest whose name was Maclean, but he might as well have been called Armstrong or Grotjohann. Her voice was soft, but it did not falter at the sound of his. Her steps were obedient as ever, but a thin thread led from her feet right back to the house by the water, giving them a gentle unerringness in the way they went.

"The Devil is on your path," he whispered threateningly and laid his hand on her arm. "I shall drive him out of your life."

But she shook her head. "God has come to me," she said tranquilly. "I only obey."

On Shrove Tuesday the two in the ferry house realized for the first time that out of the harshness of winter, hunger and hopelessness, evil was being born, directed against them. Just as every year, the villagers visited each other, disguised so that they were quite unrecognizable, glowing in all their carnival frolic with the accumulated hatred of a whole year. This time, too, they knocked so hard that the door shook on its hinges; and they did not utter the usual greeting, but stepped forward into the light of the fire, where they bowed with clumsy movements; a devil wrapped in straw, a bear, a woman. It was obvious at the first glance that the bear was meant to be Jürgen, from the wild shock of hair that fell onto his masked forehead, from the huge shoulders and the feet bound with rags and covered with fish scales. Into the bargain he carried a short oar in his hand. And it was just as clear that the woman was meant to be Marte, since she was dressed in a red fur jacket, like the one the girl wore, and had a Bible pressed under her arm.

When the devil, lurking in a dark corner, began to pull out his concertina and the first whining chord sounded, the door opened once more and half a dozen disguised figures pushed their way in, elbowing each other and grinning.

Then, to the devil's tune, the bear and the woman began their dance, which the spectators accompanied by clapping their hands and bawling. After the first turns Jürgen stood up silently and picked up an empty ladle he had been carving. Marte, deadly pale, retreated to the wall at the back of the room. They both saw that something indecent was being represented; the bear fumbled over the woman's body in a shameless manner, and the woman, apparently shrinking back, offered herself to these movements more and more obviously, until both, swaying in an embrace, moved with unequivocal gestures towards Marte's bed.

At this moment the bear received the first wordless blow with the ladle, and as his hand went into his fur as though groping for something, he was lifted up and flung against the others. Before the staggering crowd could regain their balance, Jürgen was standing in the open door, hurling them out into the snow, one by one, last of all the devil, whom he hit over the head with the concertina before be kicked it, too, over the doorstep.

All this happened with no word being spoken, unhurriedly, as the steel arm of a machine goes smoothly up and down on its bearings, but with a merciless precision of action. And only when the room was empty did Jürgen remember his fleeting thought at the beginning of the scene—that the foreign priest might have a hand in it—and with a hoarse groan of anger he rushed out into the dark. But the crowd broke up, fleeing from his hands, and he heard them running down to the river, where the way to the moor village led over the ice.

Late in the evening another carnival visitor came, on his own. This was the tailor, Mathias Südekum. A red devil's costume hung in shreds about him, his devil's tail dragged after him by a piece of cotton, and instead of the mask a white bandage was tied round his forehead, from which red drops fell. But his eyes over the sharp nose sparkled with delight, although his mouth twitched in a slight grimace as he sat down at the hearth and stretched out his right leg—

"A stick, chum," he said smiling, "I need a little stick to lean on. They hit me on the shin with the fire tongs, the dirty dogs—but there is wailing and gnashing of teeth among the blindworms, and the womenfolk are rending their garments to make bandages. Blessed are the cold, for they yearn for the smoothing iron."

"They are tearing each other to pieces already," Jürgen said gloomily. "What will happen when hunger comes?"

"What will happen, you ask, Samson by the water? They'll go to America, men and horses and chariots, to the Golden City, where the honey will flow into their mouths and each of them hopes to have six wives, so that on Sundays he can sit and take his rest—And you, mam'selle daisy—" he raised his head unexpectedly and stared at Marte—"will you go too, so that the water snake can warm itself against you?"

"We must harvest our oats first," she said softly.

"The oats," he repeated broodingly, "yes—a funny

harvest it'll be next year among the biindworms, mark my words. A fertile religion it is that's being made there — the Holy Ghost descending upon the girls — well, well — so give me your cudgel, you old water wolf, and then sleep in peace."

"We were at his place, too," he whispered in Jürgen's ear, outside, "the saint of the Thousand Days. That's what they call themselves, I think. We went into his temple — camp bed, crucifix, you know — and what was he doing, the saint? Tying a handkerchief round his forehead. H'm? Said he'd fallen down in the road and hit his head against the fence. I should have thought the Lord protected his saints when they fall down, eh? Bolt your door well, Samson, when you go to the timber felling. There's a whisper going around that the saint has an appetite for white girls and that they'll appoint a midwife in the autumn, in both villages."

Jürgen said nothing. He only clenched the fingers of his left hand, and since he had forgotten that he was supporting Südekum's arm between these fingers, he was startled when the tailor gave a yell.

"No, not you," Jürgen said, confused, "I was forgetting — yes, get home safely now — and don't go past my goatshed, the otter stake's there — the wolf has been around."

Mathias hobbled away, smiling. "If you catch him, Samson, the wolf, I mean, then into the river with him, under the ice with the wolf — very quiet down there and very dark, for the wolf — "

The next day after the midday break, when Jürgen

went back to the big pine which they were felling, the blade of his ax stuck fast in the trunk and the handle came away in his hands. When he raised it to his eyes, he saw that it was sawn half way through, close to the blade. He looked round slowly for his two mates in the working party; but they were putting away their coffee bottles, and it took them a long time, for their fingers seemed to be stiff from the hard frost. They were smallholders, men of his own age, quiet, slow, heavy people from the green village. He had never had any quarrel with them. He thought about it for a while and remembered that Jonas, the elder of the two, had not been about when he and the other one had been sawing through the pine trunk.

He pulled the ax out of the wood, took his saw and haversack and went to the foreman. "Please can I work in another party," he said, lifting the handle of the ax slightly.

The foreman cursed and wanted to have the thing investigated at once, but Jürgen asked him not to do that.

"The frost has made them all a bit queer," he said, "and they haven't much to eat at home, so they get funny ideas, you see."

So Jürgen joined another party, strangers from distant villages, who were glad to have the giant with them. For they were doing task work. But in the evening, when the trees cast blue shadows under the yellow sky, and they were packing up their things, he held Jonas back by his arm and waited in silence until the other mate, after an uneasy glance back, had vanished along the patch into the thicket.

"Why did you do it?" he asked, worried.

At first the other denied it, with many oaths and curses, as was the manner of speech there. But when Jürgen let the saw drop from his shoulder and laid his right hand quietly on him, he confessed everything. Yes, the saint had told him. Not to saw the ax through, no, but that he was the Devil lurking on the road to the Golden City, and that he had snatched a soul from God, the soul of the girl whom he had forced into lewdness, so that she should not escape him any more. And that God would reward those who drove the Devil out of this countryside.

"So that's it," was all Jürgen said and dropped his hand again. "You knew my father?" he went on after a while, "and my father's father, and you know that they never did any harm. And now the saint comes and says that a devil is living among you, and so you collect firewood to burn him—a man can stand in water his whole life long, and then someone comes and says that he's not standing in the water but in the fire. Oh yes, you shout, all of you, *Of course it's fire, can't you see that?* A dog is cleverer than you are. He lifts his muzzle and knows that water isn't fire—and he doesn't know anything about God and the Golden City."

But Jonas only shrugged his shoulders sullenly and went away. He turned round a few times to see whether perhaps he was being followed, but Jürgen lifted his saw onto his shoulder again and set off slowly on his own path, which led away from the others through the forest.

In the evening Jürgen went to the pastor and asked to have the banns put up.

»» ««

On the way back he looked aside and saw the light in the prophet's cabin. He hesitated, because he could not think of the words that he should say, but then, after all, he pressed down the latch. The door was locked, and a voice asked who was there. He was about to turn away, but the voice held him back. Again he pressed on the cold iron, but now the voice was silent, and this silence behind the door drew him like a vortex. So he put his shoulder to the gray wood and with a slight movement pressed the lock out.

A curse in a strange language received him. Maclean was standing beside the hearth. He had a white bandage round his forehead, over which his black hair fell, and Jürgen thought that it was like the burial cloths in which the dead used to be wrapped in the old days, as he had read in the Bible. It confused him, and he did not know what to say. So he closed the door again behind him and remained standing where he was. He looked attentively into the white, stony face, and once more the wish rose in his mind to strangle this face and to dig it into the ground in the forest, where the nettles grew on heaps of stones. He could not speak, for with the first word he would have lifted his hands.

Nor did Maclean speak. He read in Jürgen's eyes that it would not be wise to speak, and so he retreated slowly, step by step, towards his bed. And as though they were bound together by an unseen thread, Jürgen followed him soundlessly, step by step, until the table with the crucifix on it stopped him. Beside the crucifix the lamp was burning, and in its light lay the pictures of the girls, the pictures with which Maclean was accustomed to play as if with cards.

They lay there, one beside the other, each half covering the next, and where the faces ended, the big Mormon Bible was laid on top of them, so that nothing was to be seen of the bodies. It looked as though the faces were growing out of the Bible.

Jürgen did not bend down. His body was like a frozen tree when he saw these pictures, and his heartbeat became so heavy that it made his lips gray. He wanted to turn round quickly and rush away—but then, after all, he looked from picture to picture. There were the faces of strangers, and then a row of girls from the village. But one was missing. He looked around in the bleak room, but apart from the hearth, the bed, and the chair, he could not see anything.

Again he looked at Maclean, and his glance touched the crucifix, at the feet of which the pictures lay. He stretched out his hand and picked it up. It was a heavy crucifix, cast in lead, and Jürgen thought that one would be able to kill a man with it, without laying hands on his infamous body. And while he was swallowing down this thought like bitter spittle, his hands pressed round both ends of the crucifix and bent them, so that tiny cracks broke open in the gray body of the Saviour.

He stared down at what he had done unconsciously, realized where his thoughts had been, and horrified and filled with confusion he put the bent cross back on the table. He opened his lips, but he said nothing, turned round without looking at the saint again, and went out, bowed and humble as after a lost fight.

On the doorstep he ran into a woman's veiled figure, which started back into the darkness with a cry. It was this cry that roused him. He looked around again as if in a strange forest and then went slowly down the road towards his house. 'No word,' he thought, still bewildered, 'both of us, no single word—at the first word I would have been a murderer—the cross saved me—' But a dull anxiety rose in him like mist. For he had broken Christ, and the body had sprung oper with gray cracks, and perhaps, in the night, blood would drip out of the cracks, a whitish blood, as from wounds breaking open again.

He found it difficult to tell Marte about the banns, and he put it off until he had chopped the last bit of firewood.

"Perhaps it was stupid," he began, "and I should have asked you."

She stopped the spinning wheel and looked up at him. For the first time his eyes met hers without wavering. And for the first time he looked at her face as at a picture one holds in one's hands that cannot defend itself. 'Like the Mother of God,' he thought and once more felt startled at what he had done.

She blushed a little under his gaze, and in this blush, although it was not the first one between them, for the first time the sweetness of their love really penetrated the numb incredulity of his soul. He was startled, like somebody beneath whose feet the earth crumbles and who falls through, and suddenly, as in a fairy tale, is standing in a bright meadow. She had been near him for almost a year, her smile, her way of talking, the movements of her body, she had been with him as much as human beings ever can be together. But all this had happened as in the darkness of night, a frail dream, a mistake perhaps, a vision of the second sight. And shyness and shame had lain upon him, as though he, a beggar, had given himself out to be a king's son and let her go on believing that he was one.

And now he looked at her without constraint, the way he looked at a bird or into the chalice of a flower. It was as if he had opened his face, and she did not withdraw from what was revealed there; she only blushed, but her eyes were moist with happiness. He saw the long eyelashes and could not understand how anyone could have such lashes. He saw her mouth and realized that this mouth had kissed him. He saw her arms and remembered that they had held him. He was so overwhelmed that against his will he groaned.

"What is it, Jürgen?" she asked quietly. "What was stupid? And why are you looking at me like that?"

"So—beautiful," he said breathlessly, "you're—so beautiful."

She was not in love for the first time, but she trembled at his clumsy words, and for a moment the ecstasy of her power passed over her soul like the wind passing over a tree. Then she stood up and huddled on the floor between his knees, her arms resting on them, and looked up to him.

"You were frozen, Jürgen, my dear," she said softly, "and now your ice is broken—it will be sweet to be at home in you."

Carefully he laid his hands round her face. "I was blind," he murmured, "all blind—a young dog with worried furrows in its face, dodging away from life—and now I see you—and I don't make you tremble as if I were a wild wolf? I'm rough and the children laugh at me—but you—you say 'my dear' to me—what good am I, why should you call me that?"

She smiled tranquilly. Gold sparks rose in her eyes and made them deeper, like a lighted room. "It's like this, Jürgen, you're a child, good and gentle like a child. And you're a man, strong and brave as a whole village. And you're a wolf that lifts and carries one like a lamb, and there's no resisting, only sweet dying under your mouth."

"You talk like something out of the Bible," he murmured, listening, "like in the fairy tales—no one in my life ever spoke like that, so that it breaks your heart—I was timid as an animal that stays in the bushes, but now you've called me and play with me, and there's nothing to be frightened of on the meadow where you play—I went to the pastor, Marte, and told him about it, about the banns."

She gave a little cry, in a high voice, like a bird in a dream. Then she sat on his knees, pressed against his chest. Now she wanted to have a child, a living creature that would hold her fast to this earth. The Golden City—there was still time for that—perhaps they would go there together some time—but first the child. She would become peaceful and would not be frightened any more—a little wolf that would drink from her life—

And it was in this night that Jürgen heard that his hopes had been blessed.

Maclean heard about the banns the same day they were read from the pulpit. He stood in the forest all day, staring at the ferry house. Once he saw the fisherman go down to the ice and stride from hole to hole, and turn back again. Once he saw Marte come out of the door and go to the shed, in her red fur jacket and without a scarf on her head. He bit into the fir twig that hung in front of his face, and only the bitter taste of the bark and the resin brought him to his senses again. Not until dusk, when a wolf began to howl in the thicket, did he return to his cabin.

The next evening, when Jürgen came home from the forest, he saw a heavy broad track running along the palings round the yard. The moon was high, and Jürgen saw that these were the prints of wooden shoes, such as the villagers wore stuffed with straw, during hard frost. He straightened up and looked over the yard. The blue light sparkled on the snow, and the shadows of sheds and cottage were cast on the ground so sharply that the edges looked as though they had been trimmed with a knife. He saw light in the little window of the shed, and he ran along the paling to the next shadow. The snow squeaked faintly, although his feet were bound with rags, as was the custom among the timber workers.

So dazzling was the light that he almost stumbled over a figure standing upright but slightly tilted, leaning against the wall of the shed, the hands pressed against the wood. At the same moment he saw the arms of the trap sticking out of the snow like an open pair of scissors and felt his foot strike against the taut chain with which it was anchored. A wild, glowing joy shot up in his heart and robbed him of breath.

It was Maclean. His eyes were shut. He was motionless, and at this moment breathless too. He would not have looked different if he had been leaning against the wall of the shed like that all through the winter. Only tiny drops of sweat on his forehead showed that he was alive. Jürgen bent down and saw how it had happened. The wood of the right shoe was crushed as in a vise, but it had held. The iron arms held the foot only, and the point of the bottom spike alone had penetrated the leather. Jürgen passed his finger round the spot where it had struck, and raised it to his eyes. It was moist and dark red. But that was all. It was as unlikely as a miracle.

This took away his anger, until he thought of the light in the goatshed. He had to take hold of the latch twice before he could open the door. The lantern stood on the little fodder box. In the corner Marte was kneeling in the straw, her arms round the animal's neck. Terror was frozen on both their faces, and when Marte opened her lips, he had to bend down before he could understand that she was asking about the wolf. No, she had heard nothing, only the iron slamming shut and something falling against the wall, no other sound. But Grita had been moaning just like that other time, and so they had been waiting for him.

He helped her to her feet and stroked her hair. "It's nothing," he said awkwardly, hiding his bloodstained hand behind his back. "Only the shoe was caught in the iron, and a bit of flesh — it's a miracle — "

"What — whose — shoe?"

He tried to smile. "The prophet, yes — he was coming to see you — Come, you must help me."

When Maclean heard the second footsteps, he opened his eyes. His gaze was fixed rigidly and somberly on her face.

"I was bringing you letters," he said slowly, as though his voice were freeing itself from the ice, "from over there — they have written that we are to come — all of us — I did not know that traps are laid for the messengers of God — "

"It was for the wolf," she whispered. "It was here — months ago — "

"It is always here," he murmured and shut his eyes again.

Jürgen pressed on the spring with all his weight, but it was dangerous, and if he slipped there might be an accident. "The vise," he muttered and hurried to the toolshed.

"I'm sorry," Marte whispered. "Does it hurt? Did it hit you?"

Again he opened his eyes, and the blue moonlight lay

uncannily in the deep hollows. "It is not the blood," he said. "But he, over there, breaks my crucifix and you deny God. Will you confess?"

"Yes," she whispered, "What is it about the crucifix?"

"Tomorrow?"

"Yes."

"Do you swear it?"

"Yes."

When the vise pressed the spring down, the iron arms opened and Maclean pulled the bloodstained spike from his foot without a sound. The snow turned red where he stood, and he swayed as he turned to go.

"Come in, so that we can bind it up for you," Marte pleaded.

He turned back once more. "We?" he answered, and his lips twisted as though he were trying to smile. "There are things which cannot be bound."

Then he went off along his old tracks, slowly, upright, without limping.

Jürgen took the trap indoors and set it once more. Now and then, between two movements, he forgot his work and stared broodingly into the fire. Sometimes too he raised his head and listened unobtrusively. But outside only the ice screamed on the lake when a cleft sprang open from one side of the forest to the other. It sounded as though a steel cable were tearing apart.

"And supposing it had killed him?" Marte asked, as she was pulling off her stockings.

He did not look up. "Perhaps it would have been

better for him," he said after a while. "A trap is merciful— and there are worse things—"

In the night he heard her weeping softly, and he laid his arm round her until her face lay on his shoulder. Then she became quiet and fell asleep, but for a long time he lay with open eyes, over which the brows were drawn together. A fox barked nearby, beyond the fields, and the moonlight climbed slowly up the wall, dissolved into a narrow, fiery streak and went out as suddenly as if a light had been extinguished behind the chink of a door.

»» ««

"It's nobody's business," Marte said sullenly. She was sitting on the chair beside Maclean's bed, but she had not taken off her jacket and had only pushed her kerchief back on her head.

He was no longer wearing the bandage round his forehead, but the edge of the scar was still red. The wound was straight with two small scars forking from it, like a twig with two alternate leaves. The whole time Marte could not help thinking that it was the imprint of a crown of thorns. She could see from the color of his eyes that he was feverish, and the compulsion to be sorry for him made her harder and more determined than she meant to be. 'He needn't have gone to bed,' she thought, 'when he knew I was coming.'

He lay without stirring and looked at her. She waited for him to lower his eyelids for once, but they were motionless, as though frozen. And although she felt that her roots were in the ferry house, and reached to her through the snow, not cut by anyone, a growing paralysis came over her from this lidless, staring gaze.

"You wanted to confess?" he asked, tonelessly, as people speak in their sleep.

"I said that we are going to marry and that I—that I am his—there's nothing else to confess."

"But how did it happen? When? How often?"

"That's nobody's business," she repeated.

Dusk was beginning to fall, and every trace of light still remaining seemed to gather in the white face above which the red scar ran. On the road someone passed, pulling a sledge along behind. Perhaps a woman who had been collecting firewood. The snow creaked, the runners scraped over a stone, then again in the distance—then everything was still again.

"Perhaps you would prefer to leave the congregation?"

"No."

"We had one over there who left the congregation. She refused herself to the priest before marriage—like you, and then she left. Her first child was blind. The second ate its own dung and crawled on all fours. There were other examples too, many. Human beings thought they were cleverer, but God was the clever one—"

"That doesn't come from God," she whispered, white to the lips.

"Then it comes from my prayers," he said, just as quietly.

She felt her blood turning cold, coagulating and freezing. Deep within her body she felt the gray breath of a sheet of ice, there where the miracle of birth was quietly coming about. She closed her eyes, but then she saw all the more clearly and inexorably the image of the blood freezing and how under the child's closed lids a gray, cold skin spread over the eyeballs. She fell on her knees, with rigid joints.

"Don't pray," she whispered, her forehead on the edge of the bed. "Pray for my blindness, for my death, but not for that."

"Obey."

"No."

"Then I shall pray, morning and evening and once in the night, and—"

She struck out with her clenched fist, out of the midst of her rigidity, without seeing where she struck. Then she jumped up, and before he could seize hold of her dress, she was at the door.

"Both of us will pray," she said, "morning and evening and many times in the night. But you will be praying to the devil, and I shall be praying to God, that he may strangle your devil."

In the night Jürgen was wakened by two hands being laid on his eyes.

"What's the matter?" he asked.

"Kill him," she whispered.

He knew everything, immediately. She felt his eyelids flutter under her hands and lay back quietly.

"It's a sin," he said after a long while. "It's not right to think a sin."

"No—it was a bad dream—go to sleep now."

At the end of March, as Marte was standing in the

yard one evening, looking towards the forest to see if Jürgen were coming yet, the rooks were flying to the trees where they settled for the night. They were cawing so loudly that Marte looked up, and she saw that they were rolling about in the air, as though in play, so that between two strokes of their wings the dark bodies revolved once on their own axes. Then she knew that the thaw was coming, and she drew in a deep breath of the cold air. In the evening, by the hearth, she felt the child stirring for the first time, and with the sweet trembling that shot through her, right to her toes, the certainty came to her that everything had been a bad winter's dream. She let the spinning wheel rest, bent forward with closed eyes and listened.

"Can you hear something?" Jürgen asked.

"Yes—it's thawing—"

He looked at her guardedly and went to the window.

"There's a halo round the moon, but it hasn't got that far yet."

"The ice, Jürgen," she said, smiling, "the ice is melting."

She did not sleep, for it came again in the night. There was a sleep-walker within her, and she lay very still, to guard him. The wind had sprung up, blowing in irregular gusts over the earth. She knew by the sound that it was an easterly wind. But at midnight the first scream came from the forest—a tree in which the ice was breaking. She had her hands folded over her breast, in which there was a faint aching pain, and she pressed her fingers together, trying to make sure that she had not been deceived. But a second cry answered, far off, like a shot coming from one of the houses. Jürgen stirred in his sleep, as if it had called for him from far away. She turned her face very quietly, until her hair touched his shoulder, and lay now in a profound, ever mounting happiness, soft and relaxed as though dissolving after long stiffness. There was another shot in the forest—now a thin crack was breaking through the icy skin on the young eyes. The wind blew against the roof and puffed down the chimney into the clay hearth—now a fine, gray floe was splintering, crumbling at the edges, letting the blue of the eyes free like liberated water, the hands were lifting to wipe away cold sleep and they pushed softly against the warm wall of her womb. Oh blessing from God that came with the mild western wind over blindness and freezing—a fiber snapped in the oak outside the door, like the string of a fiddle, and over the lake a white, jagged crack split with a roar.

"You will rise—" she whispered, "you will rise from the dead."

Before dawn it began dripping from the roof, at first in single drops, at long intervals, so feebly that it might have been been the worm in the wood. But then it came faster, louder, more certain. The melting snow thudded from the fir branches, and whenever the wind stopped for a while the quiet unrest of the earth rose to her ears. Now there was no more doubt; and when the first wan light made the window stand out against the blackness of the wall, she lay back, breathing deeply, shut her eyes and felt, on the brink of sleep, how her body seemed to be slipping away from her, as if she had already given birth and were laying her hands round the new generation into which her blood had passed.

The next day she went to the pastor, said that she wished to leave the congregation of the Mormons, and asked him to receive her again into his church, her and the child she was carrying.

Soon after that they had their simple wedding. Michael Grotjohann, he who had been called to grace, came the evening before, not as a wedding guest but as an emissary of the Mormon church, to lead the apostate daughter back again on to the road to the Golden City. He sat before the fire, miserable, frozen, with his hairless head and the crooked nose, like a plucked crow, asking, imploring, threatening and cursing.

"I knew it," he said, raising his lashless eyes to his daughter, "as soon as we came here. The devil met us in the forest, and his breath smelt of the fogs of hell. He led us sorely astray, and now they have stolen your soul."

"Let it be, father," she said.

But he crouched before the hearth like a reptile, crunching his words and sorrows like a beetle in the wood, groping around him as with feelers.

"What is a fiisherman, anyway?" he nagged contemptuously. "He has scales on his hands and in his hair, and when he grows old all his joints ache. In the Golden City you would have had a golden bed. You would have borne prophets, and now they will be frogs or toads."

"Now stop this talk," she said sternly. "You weren't born in a golden bed, either—"

"Look here," he said, when Jürgen had come back from the forest, "she has left the congregation—do you know how it is in our faith? Nine nights they must kneel before the bed after the wedding and not touch each other, so that it shall become a lust of the soul and not a lust of the flesh—and now, are you going to kneel?"

Jürgen had to look at him for a while.

"Nine nights?" he asked and shook his head. "I don't think she wants to—It's—yes, it's simpler with us, you know—and she was better off without kneeling, believe me."

It was some time before Grotjohann had taken that in. His Adam's apple moved as if he were choking down word after word.

"And about the dowry," he said then, "of course there's no question of that, seeing that she has left the faith."

"Even the devil has his good points," Jürgen remarked amiably.

In the morning a pole was planted in the yard, and on top of it there hung a wreath of straw. Quickly Jürgen glanced back at the window and carried the whole thing into the shed. He undid the wreath and scattered the straw in the goatshed. Then he went to his field and pushed the damp snow aside with his hands, until he could see a small circle of dark earth. He knelt down and bent over the opening. Green blades lay thick and strong at the bottom of the narrow shaft. It smelt of earth, roots and forest, and behind his closed eyes he felt as if it were the same smell that came to him from Marte's hair and skin. 'A field and a son,' he thought, 'the other things come from the others – but this comes from ourselves – '

At the church door Michael Grotjohann took his leave. No, he was not going into the house of the apostates and he must hurry home, for someone was to be called to grace that evening in another congregation and he had to be there for the 'preparation,' so that he who had hitherto been without light might be softened and grace might fall into him as into a field. He should not knead too much, Jürgen suggested, for a field that got too much kneading turned into dust. Marte only gave him her hand, as to a stranger.

There was no disturbance, only that the pastor had to ask twice before he heard Jürgen's 'yes' so quietly did he speak. And when they exchanged rings and his heavy hand trembled, Marte bent down and kissed it. Jürgen became scarlet, and the pastor smiled very gently, without mockery, as though to a child.

"You faithful ferryman," he said, in such a way that only they two heard it.

"He's too good," Jürgen said in the evening, when they were still lying awake. "Faithful, you see, that's a big word. Christ, or Peter, or perhaps an emperor, they can be faithful – but I'm a fisherman, a simple man, and it's too much praise before you – "

But she smiled and laid her cheek on his chest.

"How it beats," she said, "like a clock in a big house—not even a child would be frightened, it beats so calmly, so—faithfully."

»» Chapter Five ««

JÜRGEN WENT TO LOOK AT HIS FERRY, which was still stuck fast in the ice, and at his boats. The water was already up to the rim, and across the river broad cracks ran crisscross, from which bright bubbles rose. Now and then the ferry quivered as he stood on it, when upstream in the distance a muffled roaring ran through the earth and a slight, creaking shudder seemed to pass over the gray ice. The storm thundered out of the forest and was like a wet, warm wall when he raised his hand into the wind.

He did not like it at all. Particularly that everything was quite still downstream. The lake ice lay firm, without a sound, and if the river were to thaw open, the ice would pile up. He had experienced it before and three times he had had to stay in the cottage attic for many days and nights, and his father and grandfather had known still worse. But then he shook his head, thinking that he had become nervous since he had a wife, and he tested the moorings of the ferry once more, pulled the two boats a few yards higher up the bank and bent down for his tools.

But in the instant that he stretched out his hand for the ice ax, he heard a faint, whining sound from beyond the ferry. It seemed to come from the earth and to fall back into it again, as if a heavy door were moving on rusty hinges. There was a fine crackling at the edge of the sound, as if something were crumbling away with a sighing movement. And at the same time, bending down still further, Jürgen saw a change in the world in which he stood. It was as if the gray river bed were lifting itself in the middle in a slight curve while the ice joints grated against both banks, and sinking slowly back to the level of a gray mirror with thin cracks running through it. At the same time a gurgling flood of dark water rose along the banks, boiling with gray bubbles, stood like a low wall along the edge of the ice, and sank back again into the depths with a suppressed moan that faded into the earth.

'I see,' Jürgen said.

He took the ice ax over his shoulder and walked quickly along the edge of the river bank, towards the invisible current. But the picture was the same upstream, a gray, furrowed face twitching slightly. By now it was nearly dark, and Jürgen's eyes watered when he tried to peer into the distance against the storm. Rooks were drifting past him, falling through the storm with outspread wings, and in the forest there was a howling of invisible voices. He covered his eyes with his hand, but river and sky merged in the pale twilight. A wall of rain passed over the moor on his left, pouring out of the clouds in dark ribbons like a heavy curtain dragging over the earth. He followed it with his eyes, frowning anxiously. And at the moment when he was about to turn away, it happened. Out of the river bed, where in the distance it merged with the earth, something gray and ponderous reared up like a jagged wall, rose soundlessly until it stood tilted, shimmering whitely in the gray air, and then sank back again quietly. It was as though a dead man had risen and lain down again. And only long afterwards an underground thunder ran beneath Jürgen's feet and branched out into little crepitations. This was the first floe rising in the current.

He ran back and tried to measure the strength of the ice at the river bank by the ferry, but when he found he could put his arm down into the ice hole without touching water, he gave it up. All the horses of both villages could not have moved the ferry from its place. Once more he stood in the dark listening for a long time; but now the ice was still. Only the storm roared and raindrops began to beat against his face. It was a warm rain, and that reassured him somewhat. But in spite of that he went round the yard in the last light and carried everything he could move into shed and house.

"What's the matter, Jürgen?" Marte asked in the evening. "Are you waiting for something?"

He shook his head, slightly perplexed. "It's all quiet," he answered. "The ice is coming — nobody ever knows how it will be."

"Oh, you faithful ferryman," she said, smiling, "it will be sure to leave our ferry alone."

He nodded, discarding some of his worry, and meditated for a long time on her having said 'our ferry.' After she had gone to bed he remained sitting there, smoked a pipe, laid another birch log on the fire, and felt how good the warmth was after the storm on the river, and the glow of the firelight, as on a Sunday. 'So long as it goes well with the oats,' he thought, 'I've earned a lot at the timber felling — perhaps, next spring, a horse.'

And then he rested his head in both hands and thought about what they would christen their son and what name they would give the horse.

She was smiling in her sleep when he lay down beside her.

In the night he woke. It was still dark, but he felt that it must be very nearly morning. The storm was raging so furiously that he thought he felt the faint shuddering running through the wood of the bed. He lifted his head and listened. His heart was thudding as if a nightmare had been lying on his chest, but between the pulses of his blood he heard something else behind the storm as well. The storm roared in the chimney and howled in the fire behind the yard, but behind its thundering was a creaking, grinding sound, like stones grinding something between them.

He sat up, careful not to wake Marte, and heard a second sound, furtive, like water dripping into a deep jug or being drawn down into the depths in an eddy.

He did not know what time it was and how long he had been sleeping, but now he was wide awake and alert, and his thoughts ran ahead quickly and systematically to everything that had to be done. The boat, the goat, the ladder, beds, wood, bread, flour, the little stove from the shed—nothing must be forgotten. 'The field—' he thought, and that was a quick, dull feeling of pain, but he had already thrown aside the blanket carefully and put his feet on the floor boards.

He was standing up to his ankles in water. The cold struck up to his heart like lightning, and for a moment he stood chilled and stunned. 'Well—' he thought, 'just look at that—' Then he woke Marte.

He had thought of everything, and he worked without talking, in an organized way, without haste. Nothing slipped from his hands, no journey was made twice, no glance was wasted on things not worth looking at. The water was there, and in the water he was at home. As soon as the beds, stove, wood and lamp were in the attic, Marte had to go up. When she resisted, he took her in his arms like a young animal and carried her up the ladder. "The child," was all he said. "Ice water isn't good for children."

She lay among her pillows, pale but without fear, and

every time he came up the ladder, with the goat, a sack of flour, or a heap of wood, she smiled at him.

"The lake hasn't broken," he said once, "that's why it is. And the bridge is blocking it. But if the storm drops, it may perhaps be all right by evening."

Then he ran down to the river to fetch the boats. Now it was broad daylight, and the river was a roaring shaft of ice. It had not thawed on the surface, but had broken up from below. Whole walls suddenly rose out of the cauldron, stood up, thundered as they cracked at the edges and smashed down again with a burst of froth. The black water was boiling with white bubbles. Away beyond the ferry a white mountain towered up, droning like an earthquake. Afar off, where the river made a sharp bend and disappeared into the woods, stood a shuddering wall over which the single floes shot out in white discs.

The water reached beyond his knees, and there was no dry land within sight. The forest stood up as though over the horizon, and both villages lay like drawings on a sheet of paper. In pauses in the storm the reeds by the banks hissed as though under a scythe when the driving floes sliced them through. The sky in the east was white with pale spots and streaks. The sun could not be seen.

He tried to sling a second steel cable round an iron clamp on the rim of the ferry. The ice cut into his hands, but he was able to make the knot fast and to tie the other end round the nearest oak. Then he hauled the two boats up to the house. The current was already pressing against his body, and he had to walk sideways, the towing rope over his bent back, in order to hold the boats steady. The water away from the river bed was free from floes. The storm cast up bubbles on the surface, but when Jürgen bent down, he saw that the water was furrowed and that the force dammed up by the ice was driving the whole sheet of water to both sides with immense pressure. 'The pastor will have to speak to the soldiers,' he thought, 'for them to come and blow it up—ice won't come on the field anyway—the forest's in the way.'

Now and then a branch drifted past, or a piece of turf, or a bunch of snapped rushes. They looked forlorn on the huge expanse of water and more menacing than big icefloes would have been. The fence was already half submerged. The lower end of the plowshare was touching the water, and whenever some flotsam grazed it, it gave out a thin, ringing sound that seemed to rise out of the flood like a bird and then fall back again. Once, when Jürgen paused in order to wind the rope once more round his hand, it seemed to him that the water had stopped flowing, but that his whole homestead, cottage, sheds, oaks, and fence were rushing soundlessly past him. He was startled and realized that his eyes were tired from the flowing dissolution of all visible things; and he did not stop in his work again until both boats were in the lee of the house and he had pulled the ropes up a ladder and in the attic window.

All this time Marte lay still and without fear on the bed that Jürgen had made out of pillows for her. She had been up for a little while, to light a fire in the little iron stove and to put on coffee for him. She had extinguished the light and looked out of both the little windows from which she first had to wipe away the cobwebs. It was a threatening and magnificent picture for her; she had never seen anything like it before. But it did not go further than her eyes. She saw Jürgen working at the ferry and was without fear for him. A giant was there, striking the ice with his ax to fasten a steel rope, and if he wanted to he would smash up ferry and river and forest. He had carried the fish box on his shoulders the first morning that she had been in this house, and he would take the house on his shoulders too if it should be necessary, the house and herself and the child, and walk through the water with his heavy tread and put everything down again carefully where there was no water, no ice and no storm. A faithful ferryman, more faithful than emperors and kings.

And she looked out of the window, over towards the village, which lay weirdly clear and clean on the water, and saw the cabin at the nearest end, standing somewhat to one side, close behind the clump of firs which now only held a few arms up out of the flood. But the cabin, too, only reached her eyes as a picture. She saw him lying stretched out on his bed, the jagged scar across his forehead; but only a fleeting frown passed over her brow. Let him drown, let him float, with bed and table and crucifix. All that was far away, death and human beings and the Golden City, for all life was gathered in her, in her womb that had been blessed and in which there was a stirring and a groping.

She lay down again, clasped her hands under her breast

and gazed up into the beams and rafters. Perhaps the water would stay. Perhaps for weeks and months, and the child would be born here in the loft. Just as in Noah's Ark, She thought about it, but she could not remember whether a child had been born in the Ark. Her thoughts went back lethargically to her schooldays and being prepared for confirmation, then they slipped away, to the teacher's face, to her schoolmates, to the white hands of a curate whom she had loved hopelessly from afar. But again and again they returned to the Ark and whether her child would be born in it.

And suddenly, like a cold stone falling into her heart, the realization came that the Bible was still downstairs. The pastor had given her a Bible when he had received her back into the church, and it was still lying on the shelf at the head of her bed. Her hands turned cold. She threw back the bedding, pulled on her warm skirt and stepped into Jürgen's old fishing boots, which reached right up her thighs. She ran to both the windows, but Jürgen was not to be seen. He would be angry, but she had to fetch the Bible. Or otherwise it would be as though she wanted to live without God up here.

Her body was already heavy, and it was laborious climbing down in the high boots. Things did not look good in the room. The water had already risen over the mantel, and the table was floating by the window with a slight revolving motion. In the corners the water was whispering and gurgling, as if there were a hidden way out there into which it was being drawn in little eddies. At first she shut her eyes, but then she went bravely to the corner where the empty bedstead was. The water came up to her body and was like icy bandages wrapping her legs. When she gripped the Bible in both hands, she had to let go of the tops of the heavy boots, and the water rushed in. 'I'll rub myself down,' she thought, 'then it won't matter. I'll have to put the boots away in a dark place so that he doesn't notice—'

It was difficult to climb up the ladder again. She could hold on only with one hand, and at every rung the water gurgled in the boots. Her feet were heavy as lead and quite numb.

When she had reached the fourth rung, she heard Jürgen at the door. She tried to hold on to the rungs above her, but the door was already opening. Storm, light and water rushed into the narrow room, onto the ladder and onto her. She tried to run up two rungs at a time, slipped, cried out, and fell down the ladder into the splashing water, her free hand still clutching the wood.

It was not a heavy fall. She landed on her feet, but her weak knees gave way beneath her and the water covered her up to her shoulders. Jürgen lifted her up and carried her upstairs, without a word, but his face was gray with fright. Her head rested on his shoulder, and from below she looked into his face that was covered with the sweat of work.

"The Bible," she said and stroked his cheek with her free hand. Deep emotion overcame her, and she was full of happiness and pity, and like a child, and she would gladly have remained so, high above the water, at his chest, without stirring, just borne in his arms.

He rubbed her down until her skin was burning hot, and from this abandonment too a deep happiness rose and enveloped her completely. Never yet had she shown herself to him like that by daylight, but she felt no shame under his hands. And when he had finished and asked if she were warm, she laid his hand round her left breast and only smiled with closed eyes. He prepared a stone bottle with hot water for her, put fresh wood into the stove, and pulled the lines to which the boats were tied through the window. Then he went down once more to fetch hay for the goat.

When he came back, Marte was sitting up among her pillows, with pale, drawn lips. Her hair was damp round the temples, and she had her clasped hands stretched out before her in a senseless gesture.

"The child," she whispered, "Jürgen — the child."

He dropped the hay where he stood. His arms hung down and his shoulders slumped forward heavily. His first step was towards the boats, but she called him to her and clutched his arm with both hands.

"Don't go, Jürgen," she whispered, "don't go — nobody'll come with you — nobody's to know, only us two, only us two — they'll put a spell on my womb for ever — don't go — do you hear?"

He only nodded, blind and dumb. The water had stolen his son, as it would steal his field. There would be nothing for him to hold in his hands, softly and carefully. The river was roaring behind the wall, and beyond the roaring echoed, high and shrill, like a chorus of children's voices, the forgotten rhyme: "Doskocil – can't do this – "

Absent-mindedly he stroked Marte's damp forehead.

"It's from the fall," he said. "Don't cry, at Christmas you'll have a baby Jesus."

"Yes," she whispered, "many children, many – with bright eyes – all blue like forget-me-nots."

But dark lines were engraved round her mouth, and her heart contracted at the realization that *his* prayers had been stronger. He must not drown, no harm must befall him, for first he must stop praying, he must take the curse from her womb.

At noon it was born. It had no resemblance to a human being, and Jürgen wrapped it in a cloth and laid it on the old loom in the dark corner. He knew nothing about all this. He just did what Marte told him to do, swaying, stunned, speechless.

Then he washed her, covered her up and sat by her until she had fallen asleep. She had not cried out at all, but he could see now that she had a different face. It was a face as after a night frost. Where was comfort for her? Was there any comfort in this world? A man did his work, but the ice came and swept the work away. A man did no harm, either to other human beings or to animals, but they sawed through the handle of your ax. He bred a child, sowing it in the willing body like corn in the earth, but the water came and took the corn seed, and only the earth remained, wrapped in a cloth, and he could not even bury it. A faithful servant, the pastor said, but what was faithfulness? Every morning the same work, every evening the same sorrows. Much sweat and a poor harvest. But the lord drives off from his manor, with two horses and a proud carriage, and the servant remains behind on his straw and waits for his return, and unharnesses the horses and has his scanty sleep, until the birds start calling in the trees. We shall begin all over again, yes, with the field and with the child. We shall have to lay new floor boards, and if the ferry is smashed, we shall build a new one. The beginning, that's what life is. Not the end.

He sat without moving, his head resting on both his fists. Marte was asleep, and he saw the quilt on her breast rising and falling. Now and then something knocked against the house, an icefloe or a tree. Then the plaster pattered down behind the wall, and a tense, whining sound went through the rafters. Towards dusk a high, ringing cry rose from the river, and after that a second one. It sounded as though a vibrating string were being tightened until it snapped. 'The ferry,' Jürgen thought. But he did not get up. He would fetch it back from the lake or build a new one. So long as wood grew in the forest, one could build ferries, one after the other.

Not until it was becoming dark did he stand up. Not until then did he notice that the storm had passed. Only the gurgling and rustling of the streaming water enfolded the house. He looked out of the window. Now the water would reach up to his neck, but if there were no pressure of the wind it would only rise slowly. He went to the loom and took the cloth. He must take it away and lay it outside on the ladder or under a rafter. But when Marte woke it must not be there any more.

He climbed down a few rungs of the ladder and looked around. The wall of the room projected into the lobby, and if he leaned far over to one side he could put it down there. He looked round for a pole on which to support himself, but he found nothing. He had to go back and fetch an oar. The outside door had remained open, and in the floating, white light he saw the pale, streaming water pushing into the house in dark eddies. The door to the room had sprung open and was swinging silently to and fro. It was as if a child were hanging onto the latch behind it, swinging it for fun. 'The hearth will have to be laid again,' he thought, 'If the pastor had some old tiles, then it needn't be clay that—'

Here his thoughts broke off. In the doorway stood the gray, vaporous, misty thing that had no face and was only a dissolving shape. Just a body that rose above the water with shadowy shoulders and that groped forward against the current with invisible arms. And when it had reached the threshold it lifted one arm and made an indistinct but somehow demanding gesture, a kind of waving which slowly dissolved and seemed to fade away. An icefloe no more than a few inches across came through the doorway, struck against the ladder, whirled around and glided through the open door into the room. It slid through the gray thing, cutting it in two just above the shoulders, and took it with it so that only the dark water remained, with little white bubbles floating on it.

Jürgen drew back his arm. He believed he had understood that the shadow wanted something, but Jürgen did not want the same. He would not buy his peace of mind with something that had grown in Marte's body. He sat on the ladder for a while longer. As always after such apparitions his knees were tired, and a cool hand pressed on his heart. All thoughts died away. A moist chill went through him, right to the marrow, like autumn mist on the river by night. A child could have pushed him off his seat, and he would not have resisted. Only the floe still drifted before his eyes, with its white edge that had cut through the shadow.

Now they did not talk much. The wind had gone, and it was as though they were in a boat with thin walls, behind which the current lapped. Once she asked if the village were still standing. Yes, it was still standing. All the houses? Yes, all of them.

At nightfall the house shook under the first explosions at the edge of the lake.

"The soldiers have come," Jürgen said.

But she only nodded. Her eyes were wide open, looking at something invisible.

"Jürgen," she said in the middle of the night, grasping his hand, "do you think that God destroys evil, by Himself?"

He had to think about it for a long time, for he was very tired from the day that was gone. "I think it's the same as with the wheat," he answered at last. "We can pull up the weeds, and it doesn't help. But if the wheat has strength in its roots, then it grows so thick that it chokes the evil."

"You mean we have to have strength in our roots? And we have to be very good, better and better every day, and then that will choke the evil?"

"Yes, that's what I mean."

But after a while she shook her head gloomily.

"God can be cheated," she said harshly. "He chokes the child in the womb."

It gave him a shock, but he did not know what to say. And then they pretended to be asleep, but they were both awake, and Jürgen thought that it would have been a good thing if instead of the little icefloe the dark priest had drifted over the threshold, lying on his back, with wide open eyes like the drowned man he had once found in the river.

Two days later they were able to go downstairs. Not much had happened. The soldiers brought the ferry back, and Jürgen washed the mud out of the room and mended the hearth. The floor boards had warped a bit, and the cellar had to be baled out with buckets. Yet the weather was warm and sunny, and it dried quickly. What remained was a scarcely perceptible smell that hovered between the walls, a smell of water, warm wind and decaying reeds. Every time Jürgen came into the room, he held his breath and hoped it would be gone. But it did not go. He burnt juniper twigs, and all day long windows and doors were kept open. But the smell stayed, and Jürgen knew that it was the shadow from which the smell came. It was the moldering of the shadow which the icefloe had cut in two across the shoulders.

While he was working, from morning until late at

night, Marte lay in the sun among her pillows. She did not move a hand. Jürgen had propped her head up, and now she stared out at the river, on which the gray ice was still drifting, and across it to the moor, where the lapwings were crying. She was not hostile to Jürgen. She even stroked his hand with two fingers, when he put her pillows right. But she was absent even while she stroked him. She lay there as if on a station platform; a strange name, a strange country, and her soul was far ahead—at the destination to which the thundering train would bring her.

She had simple things to brood on. If she had not climbed down to get the Bible, would all that not have happened? Would it have been born at its time, healthy and strong? If that was so, then she must take Jürgen to her as soon as she was well, in order to have another child. But supposing it were not so? Supposing those eyes remained on her, penetrating her, penetrating her body and piercing through right to the sleep of the fruit? Supposing they were quietly weaving the skin of blindness, illness and deformity?

What use would it be if they fled? Even to the uttermost parts of the sea? He would be able to stay calmly in his cabin, sitting by the hearth with folded hands, and from there it would go out over lands and seas, the prayer of his lips, and reach her, her womb, her fruit. And it would cease only with his death or —with her obedience.

"Bury it," she said to Jürgen the first evening.

He asked softly about seeing the pastor. But no, she

wanted no pastor. Not under the oaks, no. At the edge of the forest.

So Jürgen hammered the little coffin together and laid the bundle in it. He did not turn back the cloth. He held it in his hands for a long time before he laid it in. It was like wasted seed, and now he knew that the dead woman had fetched it. Nothing had been any use, neither the kerchief nor the ring. She had been stronger than he. Perhaps he ought to bury it at her side, but then he would be robbing Marte. By the forest it was good too. Those down below would come and take it to her. Or they would dig a passage along underneath meadows and fields up to that grave. Then she would have her rights and be quiet. She had always been quiet when she had had her rights.

He went into the house and asked Marte if she wanted to lay her hand on the coffin.

"No," she said, her face to the wall.

So he buried it under the gray pines. The spade rang on the stones under the earth, and when he straightened up to rest, he heard the birds of night calling from across the river. The water had stolen everything from him, but it was beginning to call him and draw him again to its still, dark rustling, its unfathomable being, its smell that came from the depths. He put the coffin into the deep hole, threw the soil in again and placed a cross which he had nailed together at the head of the grave. He wanted to pray, but he could not think of anything. He stood for a while, his hands clasped round the handle of the spade, watching how the shadows of the clouds under the moon crept through the forest, and then he went along the boundary ditch to the clearing where his field was.

He had not been there since the ice came. He had been afraid. But now, coming from the little grave, he could go there. He saw that the beech copse over the ditch was full of drifted hay and reeds and that the mud behind it was already dry and cracked. 'It might be,' he thought. 'The current was strong, and in the yard there isn't more than a finger's breadth—only where it didn't flow, there's more, like in the room—but it lasted three days, and it came up to my neck—'

He had narrowed his eyes so that he could only just see his way. The moon was high over the clearing, and the pale light fell on a green meadow. Jürgen's heart suddenly began to beat fast, and he ran a few paces forward to come out of the shadows. 'It can't be,' he thought, 'it can't be.' And when he was kneeling on the ground and passing both hands over the strong, green shoots, he still went on repeating the same words. But even when he opened his eyes as wide as he could, the picture remained unchanged: a green, healthy, bright field, through which a deer's track already ran across in front of him, leaving deep imprints in the soft ground. The water had not stolen his field.

He walked all round it. He talked to himself, loudly and still bewildered. He talked to the young seed, to the water that had run away, to the wind that had dried it. He talked as to a young animal that had strayed and caused him much worry and that he was now carrying in his arms, with quiet reproaches, still full of the memory of his anxious search, but brimming over with the deep joy of the rescue.

And only when he remembered the grave did he fall silent, ashamed, and then go slowly back to the house and to her who had had the greatest loss.

"It hasn't hurt the oats," he said when he lay at her side.

She turned her face to him in the dark, and from her breathing he knew that the word had penetrated her shut spirit.

"It has choked the evil," she said after a while. "You will have bread, Jürgen."

It robbed him of much sleep that she had said 'you,' and again his thoughts began to rove about an obscure danger which he wanted to get past, but which kept turning and looking into his eyes, as does an adder's head, even when one tries to come up behind it.

»» ««

There could be no sowing in the fields around both villages. Right into May the frost stayed in the ground, and after that the horses sank in up to their knees. And when they began to cast the seed at the end of May, it was done to the accompaniment of mirth and all sorts of foolery, which went from field to field and from yoke to yoke. But the laughter was bitter, and in the midst of some tomfoolery two smallholders seized hold of their pitchforks and both had to be carried off the field by their own people.

"In the autumn the papers will come," they said, when they sat outside their doors in the evening, "then that'll be the end of this, in this accursed country."

When Jürgen took one of them over on the ferry, a sinister silence lasted all during the crossing, and the coins were put on the seat instead of into his hand. Only the young boys were different, helping him with the crossings, asking about the river and the catch and then standing on the bank for a while, plucking at a twig or boring into the ground with a stick, as though something were on their minds, a common secret or a common duty. But Jürgen did not ask, and they went away with an embarrassed word.

With the first grass on the meager grazing lands, Heini came back to his shepherd's duties. He had been in town with relatives of his mother's all through the winter. They were cobblers, in whose house he had been maid, errand boy, nurse, and scapegoat for everything for which there was no other target; their burdens, anger, scorn, even the dirt and garbage.

He had become still more twisted, and his long, narrow hands looked as if they had been in the ground all the winter. He looked at Marte distrustfully, and every word that Jürgen spoke to her drove him further back into the lair of his cripple's solitude. Jürgen knew nothing about it, but once when the fisherman had gone out, Marte took hold of Heini by the hair, shook his head, bent close down to him and said with radiant eyes: "We can both love him, can't we?"

His wrinkled face became quite white. At first he

tried to free his head, but then he kept quiet, and when she had let him go he went softly out of the door and did not come back for three days. And then he was humble and obedient and faithful as a rescued animal.

They plowed together again, or they fished, and in the long evenings when he had driven the flock back to the village, they sat by the river watching the stars rise, listening to the heron screeching over the reeds, the bittern by the lake, the plover over the moor; they talked little and their souls were at leisure. Sometimes Marte would sit with them, her hands clasped round her knees; sometimes they heard her singing softly in the house, a mournful song that moved slowly and low as a dark bird over the meadows.

Sometimes Heini talked about the town and of his life with the cobbler's family.

"Horseflies, that's what they were like," he said. "Man, wife and children. But the woman was the worst. He only hit out or bawled or threw boots. But she stung and left the sting behind. The children were like devils, and when I defended myself, they complained about me and I had to apologize. The youngest was four, with a face like a sowbug. In front of that I had to kneel down and ask to be forgiven. At first I wouldn't. So she waited till he came home drunk. Then he tied me up and beat me with the strap."

Jürgen groaned in sympathy. "Why didn't you run away?"

"Where to? At home she would have scolded me—who'll take a cripple in? Once, yes, once I wanted to kill them, the whole lot of them, but first the woman—"

"Heini!"

"Yes, that's what I wanted to do. I'd taken an awl from the workshop. It's pointed and it'll go right into the heart. I went into their room and stood in the dark until I could see everything. They were breathing like wolves, and I knew they were dreaming about me and what they could do to me next day. I wasn't sorry. Not a bit. Then I went to the bed where they were both asleep. He lay by the wall and smelt of liquor, but she lay on the outside, quite comfortable. I bent right down until I saw everything—yes, and then I couldn't do it any more. Her shift was torn, they all wore only rags under their clothes. And the left breast wasn't covered, where the heart is. Yes, and it was all withered, you see, all wrinkled and miserable, and the thing in the middle was like a sore. She was dead already, you see, shrunk like a mushroom on the stove, something to be kicked away but not to be killed. She was horrid, like a yellow worm that you find under the stones. Then I turned round, and the next day it all began again. But after that it was easier. When I looked at her I saw everything and how she had been in my power. It was as good as if I'd killed her—"

"Sometimes you think things like that," Jürgen said after a long pause.

"If you think about it, it's too late," Heini answered, as though he murdered a family every day.

Sometimes Jürgen thought that everything was the same with Marte as it had been before. But on the water, when he was by himself for many hours and only the river glided past and the nets slid through his fingers, he knew that it was not the same. She was not gloomy any more. She talked as before. She even laughed as before. But in between there were pauses when she did nothing and only stared ahead at some point he could not see. Her face, too, had become different. It was like a house into which a new wall had been built. The doors were in the old places, and the window, and the nails, yet there was a new wall. She had been familiar to him as a young animal kept about the house. But now the animal had grown older and sometimes went out of the house into the forest, all by itself. And when it came back it was a different animal. There was still a breath of the forest in its tracks and in its eyes. It let you stroke it, yet perhaps it did not feel the hand at all but the wind of the clearings and the mountains. It had a wild skin, that was it. And that was how it was with Marte, too. She did not go into the forest but she had a different skin now, and Jürgen's hand was still the same.

Marte had kept herself from him for many weeks. He had believed that it was still too soon, and never asked, not even with his eyes. She was a miracle for him, and one had to wait until the miracle came. One had no right to seek the miracle. But when it came one night, it was different from before. Even Jürgen's slow blood understood that it was different. And then he knew that she did not want to have another child from him.

This lay heavy on him, and although he had his pleasure there was bitterness in it and a sad, discouraging emptiness. All he knew was that plants and animals made love for the sake of the fruit, and in dull shame he felt Marte's unfruitfulness as his own. Yet he was shy and saw that Marte's eyes became absent when he asked about it once in a low voice. Then he reminded himself that she must be given time and that it would be terrible for her to have another dead child.

When the rye began to sprout, on miserable stalks and with short ears that the people called horsefly-heads, the rumor reached him that the priest had been ambushed one night on his way home from a village and beaten half to death. Only the forester, who was out because there had been a great deal of poaching since the spring, had prevented them from making an end of him. None of the attackers was discovered. Their faces had been blackened with soot and no one had uttered a syllable during the whole happening.

Again it was the young boys who talked to Jürgen about it, and their faces wore a look as though they had found hidden treasure.

"He says," they told him, "there was one among them with shoulders so broad as only one man in the district has, you see? His mouth's been watering for a long time, and he'd like to see the wolf caught that guards the white lamb. He knows very well that the wolf wasn't there, but it's such a chance for him, you see."

"Was it because of his religion?" Jürgen asked slowly.

"No, it was because six girls from the village will be having babies this summer—they say they conceived of the Holy Ghost."

"He got caught in my otter trap," Jürgen said.

"Yes, he mentioned that too, just by the way."

"They do everything by halves," Marte said somberly when he told her about it.

He was on the water again, when suddenly he understood a second meaning in these words. He had known that the prophet was after her. But it had been as it were, in sacred spheres, and one never knew where the soul ended and the body began. One should not chase a shy animal, but let it come to rest. But now— could it be that she was the seventh? "Kill him," she had begged him in the night. But should she not have been glad of the child's birth before anything could be read on its brow?

He let the oars sink and drifted down the river. A dark eddy went with the blade of the oar, turning deep in the black water. The boat revolved on its own, grazed the reeds by the right bank and slid out on the current again into the middle. But the eddy remained, a constant companion, and Jürgen could not take his eyes from it. He looked up only when the willow roots caught the boat and glanced around like someone lost, then he rowed the long way back. He did not believe his thought, but he had to ask her. One had to have solid ground under one's feet, else one could not live. She was not guilty, but if it were so, then one could do the other half of which she had spoken. Jürgen would be slow in doing what had to be done, but he would not do it by halves like the others.

When he saw the house, the gendarme was coming up from the direction of the moor, towards the ferry.

'You come a bit late,' Jürgen thought, 'but too soon, all the same.' He did not wait for the signal, but rowed towards him, to take him over.

He was smart and well brushed, the gendarme, and Jürgen could never understand how a man could walk so stiff and straight. Even on his bicycle he looked as though his legs, which bent treading the pedals, had been borrowed and the man himself lived only in the upper part of his body. This upper part floated, immaculate and untouchable, above the twinkling, rolling, pedaling framework below, like a ruler above a subject.

"Morning," the gendarme said, although it was evening, and raised a finger to his helmet, "I want to see you, Doskocil."

Jürgen nodded, and brought him across. They stood by the ferry, and the gendarme took out his notebook and moistened his pencil at his lips. No, Jürgen knew nothing except what he had been told. Was he on bad terms with the preacher? He wouldn't know about that either, even if he had never given him a birthday present.

"Keep to the point, please," the gendarme said severely.

There was talk about his wife having suddenly left the Mormon sect—yes, and how about the matter with the otter trap? In the middle of the sentence came a sharp turn of the head and a piercing look, as though the otter trap were snapping shut and seizing the ferryman Jürgen Doskocil between its merciless fangs.

Yes, the preacher had been caught in it, Jürgen said. He would rather have caught the wolf. Did he mean to say that he had set the trap against wolves? Yes, that was what he meant. Oh—and the night in question? Alibi? Jürgen did not know what an alibi was, but he only pointed back towards the house.

"Go and ask," he said. "It's a good thing I wasn't on the water."

No, Jürgen had not been on the water. Marte declared that she had a very good memory, probably because she had always worn a kerchief on her head instead of a helmet. She received a reprimand, but she opened the window and called to Jürgen that the sergeant would be pleased to drink a dram. After this had happened, the sergeant, slightly relaxing his bearing, revealed that there was 'no incriminating evidence,' and was willing to accept a small quantity of tench for which he paid correctly even though not much. Then he mounted his bicycle again from the back, divided himself into a mobile and an immobile half and disappeared along the road to the village.

It was in this night that Jürgen asked. He lay as still as if he were frozen and pressed his fingers together until the joints ached.

"The child," he said, "look, they're talking so much about the girls in the village—that the Holy Ghost—" he groaned and held his breath, because he did not want her to hear how he was suffering.

"Well?" she said curtly. She would not help him. Nor did she want him to help her. She wanted all this to remain in her own hands. He was so heavily burdened in his daily work and in his life that no new load must be laid on his shoulders.

"I don't want to know," he went on, dropping his voice still more, "if I was the father, or the—Holy Ghost—only if it'll go on like this, without a child—only the desire—"

She lay motionless, as he did, her arms crossed under her head, her open eyes staring into the dark. A long time passed before she answered.

"You make it too easy for your wife, Jürgen," she said then, "it's not good to tell lies in the dark. You want to know, of course you want to know. You're too humble, Jürgen."

"Perhaps," he answered, "perhaps I don't want to know because I don't want to kill. If violence has been done to you, I must kill—to strangle someone with the hands isn't easy, Marte—a wolf, you see, oh yes, but a wolf can't speak."

She shut her eyes, because now it was decided.

"You'll have a child, Jürgen," she said and laid her hand on his chest. "And no one but you was the father, do you hear? I'm not lying. Only you must give me some time, you see? It's still—it's still too soon—let's live like this through the summer, just with the desire as you call it, shall we?"

She lay awake for a long time after she had heard by his breathing that he was asleep. The white light outside the window turned pink and the cranes called from the moor. 'Before they go,' she thought, 'I must ask him if he will stop praying—and if he won't stop, I must do it—the one thing or the other—and by then I must know which will be easier.'

When Jürgen went to the river, she pretended to be asleep. But when she heard the boat chain clank, she put her arms on the quilt, spread out her fingers and looked at her firm, brown hands for a long time, as they opened and shut.

Then she got up slowly, and went about her work with a set face.

Chapter Six

MACLEAN HAD SAID THAT THEY would set out in September. They would go in a steamer as big as both villages put together. And the captain's uniform was all covered in gold, so powerful was he. For the people who fetched over travelers from Europe to America were somewhat different people from those who fetched over travelers in other places. And the steamer's engine was as big as a church, all made of steel, and during the whole journey it just went 'bom bom bom – bom bom bom' without stopping for a second, and so it hauled two villages over as easily as anything. Heini recounted this with a scornful smile at the corners of his bitter mouth. That was how his mother told the story a hundred times a day, and it really must be a Golden City if it were longing for his mother.

So in the summer, the farms and smallholdings began to be sold, and the iron on the other side of the river called Jürgen often to ferry the buyers. Each time Marte stood in the doorway and looked at the strangers gravely and in silence, at those who came alone and those who came with their wives, to look at the farms and cattle and harvest. And after one or two days, when Jürgen had brought them back over the river, she turned her dark eyes away from the quiet work and looked at him, asking, "Well, did they buy?"

And then she looked away past him into the distance and nodded to herself, as if she were counting the procession of emigrants or just following it with her eyes, gravely, overshadowed by thoughts about the future, as those who remain behind gaze after a cloud of dust on the road.

It was bad bargaining and selling, because everyone in the whole district knew they were leaving the country in the autumn, and because the fields and cattle looked as though in a desert. The autumn harvest had been lost. Then they had had frost and flood. Then they had sown with mockery and laughter at a time when in other villages the rooks could already hide in the corn. And then, since Ascension Day, there had not been more than one scanty fall of rain. At first Maclean said that it was a sign from God who was calling them, for He could break houses down and build them up again and He wished to make the passage easier for them out of an accursed into a promised land. But then, when the willow shriveled up, when the ground began to crack open and toads and worms seemed to climb out of the clefts in the earth, he said for the first time, quietly and as if under the pressure of a vision, that it looked like enchantment and that he would pray to God that He might open their eyes to the way which led to recognition of evil.

"Doskocil," the tailor Südekum had said one evening by the river when he had waved to Jürgen to come through the reeds to him, "I've had one of the blind-worms over there in my clutches. With his head under water, you know, so that he got a bit black round the eyes. And I didn't let him go till he told me. I should get myself a gun, Doskocil, and load plenty of cartridges, buckshot of course. And have a beam across the door, from inside. For else it might happen that once again they feel like beating a magician to death with thrashing flails for taking the rain away from them and bewitching their cattle. Got it?"

Jürgen had walked home very slowly and been very quiet that evening. And several times in the night he had got up and gone softly to the door, and when he returned he had bent over Marte, holding his breath, as over a buried treasure for which he was troubled in his heart.

He bought no gun. The art of shooting, it seemed to him, was a cowardly art. What he did, earned and gave, went through his hands, and if they were strong enough to fell a tree they would suffice, too, to fell any man who should stretch out a hand against his life. Yet it was without resistance that he took a wolfhound which Südekum brought him back from one of his journeys, so that Marte should not be without protection; and he also laid a heavy beam across the inside of the door.

"No, there's nothing wrong," he said to Marte, "but when the earth grows evil, human beings grow evil too, and there are many about nowadays who would shed blood for a loaf of bread."

He was not afraid. He even felt with some obscure certainty that the hand stretching out was reaching for Marte and not for him, and that he was only the lock to be smashed so that the door to his wife could be opened. But gradually he was filled with a bitter sadness that they grudged what was his own, and that the beasts of the forest were more just than man.

Meanwhile the sun rose and sank relentlessly, scorching the meadows and fields. The grass turned brown, the potato plants crumbled like tinder in the hand, the corn faded as though in the gloom of a cellar. Over the moor hovered a gray, poisonous haze as if the turf were smoldering under the surface, and whenever a hot wind passed over the land a yellow wall of dust rose over roads and fields, rising into the red hot dome of the sky and turning the sun into a red disc which lost its outlines and looked like blood in flowing dissolution, blood that was slowly spreading over a yellow wound. Through the dewless nights the blazing heat of day still lingered as in a furnace. The moon had a dead face, and everything one touched seemed to throw off sparks as if it were filled with sleeping fires. The water in the river fell and over the mud banks hung a sickly smell of decay, from bubbles that rose and burst listlessly. The fish died in the fish boxes although Jürgen changed their place daily, and he had to row to town every second day to sell what he had caught. In June the first cow fell dead in the meadow, and in July the red murrain killed off all the pigs in both villages in two days.

The houses were like graves from which no one came out by day. A smallholder who belonged to those called to grace had the idea of watering his rye field, an acre and a half, with a watering can every night; but as he had to fetch the water from the well in his neighbor's yard, they kept watch by the well and beat the water carrier when he would not give way. Not until the sun had set did the people rise from their graves. Then they stood in their fields in the twilight, motionless as gravestones outlined against the glowing sunset sky. Some knelt down and prayed, some stamped on the dying corn, and once as the sun was going down, a procession passed round the dusty fields, with hoarse chanting, led by Maclean. They were carrying something with them on a bier, but Jürgen and Marte, who were sitting at their door, could not distinguish what it was in the failing light. They only saw the fists being shaken in the direction of their house. Heini told Jürgen next day that they had been carrying a distorted image of Christ and that there had been talk of the ferryman as "God's murderer."

It hit Jürgen very hard, for all images were alive in his childlike imagination, and the only time his father had punished him severely was when, as a child, he had thoughtlessly broken a young birch tree that grew on the road to the village.

"Anger's like a hammer," he said broodingly, "you can throw the hammer in the river, but that doesn't take the crack out of the broken thing, down in the river."

Days and nights he carried his guilt around with him in silence. If they came with flails and scythes, he would be able to defend himself, but if it should occur to the preacher to give them the image of Christ to bring, too, he would have to shut his eyes. Twice he turned back, but the third time he suddenly steered the boat round, as he was setting out for his night's catch, made it fast on the bank and walked quickly, without looking up, towards Maclean's cabin. He did not care whether the preacher was at home or not, whether he had guests or not. He went his way with lowered brow, and if the door had been locked he would have burst it in, like a machine rolling in its predestined direction.

But the door was not locked. Maclean, his shallow black hat in his hand, was standing so close to the threshold that the opening door struck him, and his first movement was to put his free hand into his pocket as if searching for a weapon.

Jürgen did not look at him. His eyes, accustomed to the dark, saw the crucifix on the table. He carried it to the window, and before Maclean had opened his lips his heavy hands had bent it back into its old shape. He passed his fingers over the naked body a few times, testing it, until he felt that the cracks in the metal had closed again; then he carried the crucifix back to the table, put it down carefully and remained standing in front of it for awhile in silence, his hands resting on the table, his eyes fixed on the blank shimmer of the metal.

When, as he was going out, Maclean made an attempt to step in his way, he brushed him aside with one movement of his arm without looking up, and when he stood on the doorstep said, as if the preacher were standing in front of him and not behind him:

"He was there instead, suffering for others, as the Bible says — else I would have strangled you that time — "

"You too, my friend," Maclean answered, following him out to the doorstep, "are only there instead — " His words were quite calm, without menace or hate. Jürgen did not understand them. He felt them like a chill from the back of a knife on his neck but he shook the words off, so that they fell into the void behind him, and went slowly along the path to the river. The night was hot and airless, but Jürgen breathed as deeply as if he were walking through rain. He felt as if he had found an oar again that he had lost and were now steering his boat out of the whirls in the current, straight on its course. 'They won't be able to beat me, now,' he thought.

The thin mists from the river bed parted before him, and there was the soft murmur of the flowing water and the cool smell of the depths. In his mind's eye he saw his house, Marte's hands folded over her breast, the dog sleeping across the doorstep. The thought brought a slight pain in his heart, as from rising tears, and in the heavy feeling of happiness that almost made him dizzy he bent down on the bank, picked up one of the heavy stones the falling water had laid bare, lifted it high above his head and flung it over the boat out into the river. The water splashed apart like glowing metal, the dull blow shook the whole river bed, and the boat rose and fell on the waves that circled out in wide rings across the water.

Then he stepped softly into the boat, a little embarrassed at what he had done, and started on his night's work. The whole night long Maclean's words lay muffled and uncomprehended in his mind, like a sealed letter, and without his knowing it his thoughts were fingering over the sealed meaning. His thoughts too had a second sight which went about in the dark, and the quiet, modest experiences of his inner life did not disentangle themselves slowly one by one, like the threads of a web at the touch of careful hands, but came suddenly out of a dark house like children rubbing the sleep from their eyes.

And so, in the dawn, when he was making the boat fast again at the ferry, pulling the chain through the ring with both hands, it was no surprise to him that he suddenly knew what Maclean had meant. He straightened up slowly, looked towards the house and took in the whole picture through his heavy eyes. 'No, you're not going to take my place,' was all he thought, 'not you—'

»» ««

The oats stood thick and green. Jürgen could not understand it. When he did not have to go out on the water, he could sit for hours on the driftstone that looked as if it had been shaped as a seat for the folk down below, his head resting on both hands, thinking. It might be the forest surrounding the field which had kept the oats from languishing. But other fields too, lay on the edge of the forest and were scorched and dead. It might be the unexpended mother earth that had been sleeping quietly for centuries. It might be the subsoil water, if it were higher here than in the fields. He did not know and did not understand it. He stared at the dark green plot, where there was a faint stirring now and then as if a hand were passing over the roots; and more and more, even if secretly, he cherished the thought that it might be the folk below who were looking after the oats. Perhaps it made them cooler in their dwellings, perhaps they heard the blades above them rustling like a wood, or perhaps they expected that Jürgen would leave them part of the harvest as food for the winter. He stepped lightly when he went to his stone seat, and he did not fail to bow when he stood up again to return to his house.

But one morning, long before the harvest, the oats no longer stood there. Jürgen could see the green field from the doorstep of his house, and when he took his first or his last look over the threshold, he used to look, not toward the river or into the sky over the moor where the hazy clouds always rose first, but towards the clearing in the old forest from which the only green all round glinted.

And one morning this only green had vanished. He did not rub his eyes, nor did he run, nor did he call for Marte. Slowly, with tired knees, he went along the path to the field, past the shed where the trap had been set, along the fence where he had seen the stranger's footprints that time, across the dried up meadows towards the slanting birch at the corner of the forest. His eyes were fixed on the toes of his boots, his heavy, high water boots whose leather shimmered red from being wet every day.

Only when he reached the stone he stopped and looked up slowly. The oats had been cut with sickles, close to the ground. He could see it by the irregularity of the stubble. Here and there lay a scattered blade, already shriveling and turning brown in the sultry heat of the morning. For the rest, the field was like the face of someone who had been murdered, with open eyes, shadows in the gray furrows, pain round the twisted mouth.

He sat down on the cool stone and gazed into the murdered face. Anger and hate were still asleep in his heavy soul. Thoughts were still asleep as to who could have done it. He had received a blow from an ambush, and his blood gushed into his innermost being like rain pouring from the branches of a tree when the ax strikes at the root. Dim, fading pictures rose and moved before his open eyes—the white cloth in which he had wrapped the child; the horse into whose manger he tipped the oats; the crucifix that he had bent straight with his hands; the ax they had secretly sawn through. But behind all the pictures which drifted like mist over the river, the face of the field lay motionless. And then suddenly he knew; it was not the theft nor the loss of a harvest, but that they had mown before it was time. It was the same as with the child. They had torn the oats from the womb of the earth, as the water had torn his child from its mother's womb. They had not stolen, but committed murder.

He got up and strode round the field in ever wider circles. He found a few blades between the field and the river, and knew that they had come in boats, because there were no tracks. He saw Marte coming from the house and went to meet her. She was weeping silently, without wiping the tears away, without a word. They went back together, down to the ferry, and from there they looked towards the gray village. The draw wells cut into the hazy sky like gallows. A cart was going down the village street toward the forest, and a yellow column of dust rose behind it rolling slightly at the edges, following the cart like a specter.

That evening when the dim stars had risen and Jürgen was on the water, Marte went to Maclean's cabin for the first time. She went as far as the fir thicket from where she could see the light in the little window, and knelt there in the shallow dip of ground between the low trees, where there was a smell of resin and the heat of the whole day stood still. She knelt with clasped hands, and her lips moved without her knowing the words she spoke. And after half an hour she stood up again and went slowly back the same way. Many times more that summer she made the same journey as far as the fir thicket, and each time she returned with aching limbs, which she felt were outraged from her kneeling before the dull light that fell through the window of the cabin.

The gendarmes came, searched through the whole

village, found nothing but smiling faces, drank a dram in the ferry house and departed with worried head-shaking.

»» ««

Since Jürgen had lost the field, day and night were harder to bear than they had been before. He felt as though he were living in vain, as though he were one of the empty ears of corn that hung in thousands on the scorched fields. When he came rowing up the river towards dusk, the children of both villages sat on the banks as usual, but they no longer sang. He tried to tempt them by quietly whistling to himself the mocking song of former days. But they did not answer. Gray and silent they squatted over the reeds on the banks and stared across at him, as if they were waiting for something. But he did not know what they were waiting for.

He did not know until one noon, when the dog lifted his head and the door opened softly while they were sitting at their meal. A boy stood outside, his white head hardly reaching as high as the latch, barefooted, with a gray face, and stared with big, unblinking eyes at the fish soup steaming in the dish.

"Who do you come from?" Marte asked.

He only raised his hand and pointed over his shoulder back towards the village.

"Have you a message?"

He shook his head.

"What do you want then?"

Nothing. Only the unblinking gaze at the dish.

"Hungry," Jürgen said. "Come here."

They fed him and he ate in silence, his big eyes fixed strange and shy on their watching faces.

Had they no bread? Oh, yes, they gathered birch bark in the forest because there wasn't enough flour any more.

Jürgen filled his pipe and pulled at it until his face could not be seen behind the clouds of smoke.

"You can come again tomorrow," Marte said briefly. When he pushed his chair back, something else occurred to her and she came back to the table, the plates still in her hand. "Who did you give the oats to?" she asked. "The horse?"

The boy nodded, looked once more from her to Jürgen as though waiting for the next question, and then disappeared through the door without a sound. They saw how he crept across the yard to the forest, with the movements of a thief for whom all things seem to have eyes.

The next day there were three of them. Then there were seven, and so it remained.

"They'll laugh at you, Jürgen, when they find out," she said.

But he shook his head. "Children aren't guilty." he said.

And always about noon he stood on the doorstep and looked over towards the corner of the forest, where they appeared, a shy, gray procession, like animals leaving their dens. There were some among them whom he recognized, who had thrown stones at him and sung the hateful song after he had gone by. But he pushed the bench nearer to the table for them and watched that they did not swallow any fishbones. Marte looked at him sideways now and then, saw his bright face and the clumsy gentleness of his hands, and in her thoughts, hours in advance, she walked the hard way of the evening towards the hollow between the firs, where she prayed for strength and where she became aware of her helplessness.

"Rain doesn't come," Jürgen said, "but the children come instead."

Slowly the pain of what the village had done to him was fading away. Even the field was now like a scar which burnt only a little when he knocked it carelessly. Yet he did not forget that these were other people's children; and when they were alone again Marte felt his gaze following her, mute and downcast whenever she looked at him, but always waiting.

After the meal now he often went into the forest with the children, a second pied piper with a thin, gray procession behind him. Here under the tall pines, where there was still some coolness and gold laced shadows, they felt that all that was dangerous was left behind: hunger, heat, and the smoldering hatred of the houses. Here Jürgen showed them how to find mushrooms and how to roast them over a little fire. He showed them where the bilberries had not yet shriveled and the first blackberries were beginning to ripen. He showed them how to dig up roots and hold them in their mouths in order not to feel the torments of thirst, and how to carve and shape toys out of toadstools, lichens and bark; how to whistle on blades of grass, on reeds and lime leaves, so that the deer would appear through the thickets or the young birds of prey would look mournfully over the edge of their eyries. And with all this the time passed pleasantly, until the sun cast slanting beams through the branches and a breath of coolness rose from the hollows.

And the children, at first shy and taciturn before the heavy footed wildness of his appearance, and oppressed by the memory of stone throwing and songs, saw how this gigantic figure slowly, almost with embarrassment, opened up with them, and that in the wild husk lived neither a devil nor a black man, but a magician who with his coarse hands could call wonders out of the earth, which he seemed to call up only for them. So it was not long before Jürgen Doskocil was both a saint and a devil, and it was good that both congregations knew nothing of each other, but performed their idolatry in secret.

And one afternoon Jürgen unfolded his great plan, on which he had been brooding for a long time until, so to speak, he knew in advance every stroke of the oars he would have to make. There were no scruples and none of the hesitations which he had feared. It was no longer rare for the children of the village to gather and stay out for a whole day, begging from the farmers of the countryside. They were beaten only if they brought nothing home, and Jürgen promised that they would bring plenty home.

Marte did not argue. "Some day you will be rewarded, Jürgen," she only said, "just have patience with God and with me." No, she did not want to go too. The children were a little frightened of her. She had the dog and he need not worry.

So one morning he stepped into the light boat, made a bed of dry rushes and took the sail with him. At the first turn in the river, in the willow grove, the children were waiting. They had gray sacks over their slight shoulders, just as they were accustomed to when they visited the nearby villages. They climbed over the rim of the boat without speaking, crouched down on the rushes, signaled to one another to be quiet, and were pale and as excited as though both banks were occupied by marksmen whose arrows were already on the tightened bowstrings, to pierce their ferryman to the heart.

"All clear!" Jürgen said after they had passed the first island of reeds. And then the great journey to the town began. Jürgen hoisted the sail and between scorched banks they sailed on, a fidgeting, shouting, singing crowd, looking ahead as if they were sailing across the ocean and as if what towered up beyond the lake, with misty spires in the lead-gray haze, were the promised Golden City. But before they could distinguish buildings and people, Jürgen plunged the gray map, which lay under his seat, into the water and spread it out right across the boat over the rushes and looked, with heavy thoughts, at the bodies of the sleeping children, who had fallen into exhausted dreams.

For the little town this was a queer procession that moved on slowly through many streets towards the town hall. In front went the ferryman Jürgen Doskocil, whom everyone knew—who all the town children thought lived under the water and lured white maidens down into his solitary, sad kingdom. On his shoulder he was carrying his two oars from which he was never parted, as little as a carter from his whip. And behind him, one in the other's footsteps, came the 'seven ravens,' barefooted, bareheaded, with old faces, with gray sacks over their slight shoulders. First the children, who had been playing on the shady side of the street, fell in beside them. And then the mothers came, who had been standing on the doorsteps or in the shops. And then the old retired men came too, who had been out for their morning walk, their hands behind their backs and their short pipes in their mouths. And then the servant girls came, their baskets under their arms and the front door keys in their hands. And to all the hundreds of questions that were put to the procession the children remained silent, with set faces, and Jürgen always said the same thing; "They're eating bread made from birch bark and they're going to America in the autumn, and before that they'll be carried to the churchyard."

At the town hall they stopped, and Jürgen gave them the two big oars to hold and went up the stone steps, slowly and with a heavy heart. They had been seen from the windows, and at all the doors clerks stood and looked at them and did not rightly know whether to smile at the waterman's appearance or to make sad, sympathetic faces. Then one of them, to whom the whole cavalcade did not seem officially correct, asked him in a severe, matter of fact voice, what he wanted.

Yes, he wanted to see the burgomaster, please. On

what business? On a matter of charity. That, the clerk said, was the concern of the public assistance office. But at this point one of the older clerks pushed him gently aside, saying that a thing like this was not a matter for any office but for a man who had children himself; and he took Jürgen by the arm and led him to the burgomaster.

Here Jürgen stood just inside the door, did not sit down on the chair that was offered him, looked attentively and unassumingly into the not unfriendly face with the gold-rimmed spectacles, and told, in his slow way, how the villages were starving and that something must be done for the children before they went over to the Golden City.

The burgomaster let him finish his story and then said that the county council had decided at their meeting the day before to help the villages with food, and that the town would take part in this action, and so he could return without anxiety. For the seven whom he had brought with him, food for the journey would be provided. And then there was one thing the burgomaster wanted to know, just why precisely he, who was known to be a reserved, quiet man, had undertaken this expedition. To that all Jürgen could answer was that it was to still waters that young animals came to drink, and when the water was all drunk up, then the earth must cry out so that others might know.

The burgomaster went down with him to where the seven were still standing, huddled together, the two oars planted upright in their midst like flagpoles. He remained standing on the stone steps for a long time, looking at the children, and then said to those gathered round about that here were the little ambassadors of a great want, led by a truly merciful man who was a simple fisherman like Peter, the Lord's disciple; that the townspeople should bring to the town hall whatever they could spare in the way of foodstuff so that it could be distributed in the villages during the next few days; and over and above, that this very day they should take something to the boat for the seven before they set out again, so that the children might know that even in the town people loved their neighbors as themselves.

He said it simply and well, so that the women shed tears and the old retired men pulled hard at their pipes. He thanked Jürgen again, suggested that he should not stand in the hot sunlight of the square any longer with the children, and then, with a mute gesture, required the crowd not to yield to mere curiosity any longer, but to do what he had asked.

Jürgen had to explain where his boat lay and when he wanted to start again. And then his seven children disappeared into the crowd, drawn away by hands, carried away on arms; and soon he stood alone with his two oars on the unshaded market square, a little tired from the stir of the last hour and a little sad that they had taken the children away from him and that now he was once more nothing but the ferryman who had fetched over his travelers.

About noon they came back, one after the other. Their faces were distorted with happiness, their sacks were full, and besides that the boat was loaded with potatoes and flour, bread and sugar, so that now they really set out as though across a wide sea, with hoisted sail and waving hands, towards a distant, undiscovered shore.

They arrived, since Jürgen had to row against the current, only towards evening, unloaded the boat at the same spot in the willow grove, agreed to send two messengers to the villages after half an hour, and swore a great oath not to say anything about Jürgen and to tell a fairy story about a strange boat having taken them to the town.

"If they knew it was me" he said to Marte, "they might throw it away and beat the children."

"They would eat it first and then beat you," Marte answered. "Have you ever seen water flow up hill?"

But the secret escaped the very next day. They were lying at the edge of a moor meadow and had decided to build a hut of twigs and moss, so that they should have a house for rainy days to come like the seven dwarfs in the fairy tale. And while they were beginning to collect branches and cushions of moss, little Michael, a smallholder's child, gave a piercing yell and rushed out of the wild rosemary bushes, his arms outstretched in a gesture of terror.

"An adder!" the others cried. "It bit him."

It made no difference that Jürgen killed the snake with a stick he had picked up on the meadow. And it made no difference that he dropped the stick and folded both hands across his chest. He knew what would happen, and watched the children for a moment as they left Michael and rushed off through the pine wood crying and shouting. A thought shot through him that the fear of harm is stronger than any love, and he felt the thought as a bitter taste on his lips. Then he picked the child up and carried him into the shade. On the bare left ankle he saw the two red spots which were rapidly turning blue.

"Don't cry, Michael," he said, "It only hurts for a minute." He knelt so that the child could not see his hands, and with a swift movement the point of his knife cut through the blue spots. Even before the child could cry out he had pressed his lips to the wound and was sucking the streaming blood.

"I'm drinking all the poison out," he said then. "Nothing'll happen, and Jürgen can stand it all right."

The child looked at him with blue shadows under his eyes. He could not cry any more, he saw red blood on Jürgen's lips, and his face quivered repeatedly. Jürgen bandaged the leg under the knee with his red handkerchief, pushed a pine twig under the bandage and twisted it tight. Then he took the child in his arms and went through the forest with long, even strides. He did not run because he remembered that shaking was not good for such wounds.

When he saw the field glinting between the tree trunks, he was startled by the blazing sun and the nakedness of the empty space between himself and the village. He made a detour round the fields, always in the shade of the trees, until he reached the village from the other side. Michael's cabin was the last in the row, and from the forest he could see that the street was filled with people; he heard a woman's voice screaming, high and penetrating, and he felt that there was no good in what had happened. From behind a hedge he came into the yard. The parents were not there, but the grandmother was standing outside the door, wringing her hands.

He handed the child over to her. She tore him from his arms, and her eyes filled with hate.

"Leave that till later," he said, "Put sour milk on the place and give him some potato brandy. It isn't bad, for I sucked the poison out."

The child opened his eyes, the lids still trembling, and said slowly; "Yes, he drank my blood—his lips were all red—"

Jürgen wanted to lift his hand to stroke him again, but he did not dare because the child's words depressed him. It might be that he meant well, but it might also be that he would push Jürgen's hand away in horror.

So he left the yard quickly, going back the same way past the hedge, and was in the forest before the woman had called the parents in from the street. There he walked slowly and wiped the sweat off his forehead. And as the edge of the forest was too bright for him he turned aside from his path further and further in among the trees, and stopped now and then and looked dumbly at his hands. He felt as if he had smashed something and were now senselessly carrying the broken pieces with him.

The whole story would come out now, all of it, about the meals and the games in the forest and the trip to the town. They would beat the children and never again allow them to come to him. Michael would get well, of that he had no doubt, but he would not come either and it would not be long before they were standing by the river again and throwing stones and singing hateful songs. They were an alien stock, which one could bend down like a willow wand, but as soon as one let it go it sprang back, and the boat drifted on down the river.

A heavy weariness overcame him. He was sitting on a tree stump, his head resting in his hands, watching two ants dragging a dead caterpillar. At each blade of grass the booty slipped from their grasp, rolled over and lay like a brown coffin on the floor of the forest. And each time they began again with their hopeless task, and each time the burden was moved on the breadth of a blade of grass.

He stood up only when the sunlight was slanting through the branches. The ants had progressed one pace in hours, and before he went he lifted a branch that lay in their way. He felt a little ashamed, and when he thought of Marte and his nets he hurried back across the forest like a child that has stayed out too late playing.

"I dare say there's no harm done, Jürgen," Marte said in her thoughtful way. "It's not good to play when the forest's on fire—don't come back too late tonight."

It was the first evening with heavy clouds over the moor. Silently out of the gray haze rose gray mountains with red streaming edges, drawing close together, closing in over wan rifts and becoming a single, high, veiled wall that stood still and silent at the horizon. The birds were flying low over the river without a sound, the horseflies stung until Jürgen's hands were covered with drops of blood, the fish were leaping out of the river, making white circles everywhere, and in the reeds two pike were striking heavily on the blackish water. The alders were wan in the last light, and at each breath of wind the reeds talked with their many voices.

"Might be a storm coming," Jürgen thought. "That'd be good, and the people would become better in the rain."

He spread out the nets in the quiet creeks and backwaters. The string of the nets rustled down, pallid, into the black depths, and each lead weight as it struck against the edge of the boat echoed among the dark alders and the banks of reeds rising from the water. No bird's voice could be heard, neither over the moor nor in the dark meadows. The whole countryside was like a morgue with drawn blinds and a cloying smell, and only the current, moving softly through the creeks, gurgled and sounded and moaned among the reeds.

When Jürgen had cast the last bownets, he stayed a while longer on the dark creek from where one could see across the river to the moor and the wall of cloud above it. The boat, pressed against a bank of reeds, lay still and only the rushes grazed against its side, like the rustling of paper being furtively wrapped round something. Jürgen sat in the stern, the oar in front of him over his knees, and now and then a drop from the blade fell into the water with a clear tinkling and a dull echo, regularly, like water dripping from a gutter.

He was very tired, but his blood was quite calm, and the great hush of the landscape smoothed everything out, thoughts, cares and wishes. He was at home amidst this country, in the smell of water, alders and grass, in the dark, heavy current that bore everything along. He was so much at home here that the goat-owl, swooping up and down over the water, settled on the edge of the boat, a dark, slight bundle from which a monotonous, melancholy song rose. Far behind the forest a cart was moving through the night, and the carter's slow, sad chant ascended from the dusty track, filling all space between his road and the veiled stars, no words, only the gentle, wide curve of a tune that sank fading down to earth again, as a bird sinks on outspread wings, gradually leveling out into the distance until it was lost in the dark.

The fish were still leaping, and from time to time a bluish light played over the black, polished surface of the water. Then it flickered over the reeds, touched the leaves of the alders and died out, wiped away by some dark hand. Long, very long afterwards, a dark sound rose up beyond the moor, as though someone were walking over a vault. But it might have been a distant bittern, too, or a heavy cart crossing a bridge far beyond the moor.

Slowly Jürgen dipped his oar into the water. He would have liked to sit there all night, feeling the cool dew on his forehead; but Marte had asked him not to come home too late.

When he pushed out into the river, close under the dark bank, a branch snapped and a bird gave a cry in its sleep. It was a faint sound and passed quickly, but in the soundless abyss of the night it broke the silence so sharply that Jürgen started and stared into the dark, with lifted oar. "It's nothing," he thought, "an otter treading on a dry twig." But now he felt as though someone were walking beside him, along the bank, from tree to tree, barefooted, with an evil, lurking face. And he rowed fast and breathed easily only when the house under the oaks apeared, with its dim light shining quietly behind the panes.

Then the light went out and the stars rose. The dark wall climbed higher and higher. Blue flames shot over the edge of it, tearing forest and river and fields out of obscurity and then letting them fall back into the bottomless pit. A slight breeze passed once along the river, bending the reeds, turning each leaf, reaching the ferry and then the tall rushes. And then it was gone, and all doors closed soundlessly behind it. And long afterwards thunder went over the world, still very distant, but speaking, and its dark words dropped heavily out of the vault, one by one.

Marte was the first to hear it, and straight after that the dog lifted its narrow head. Running, stumbling footsteps were approaching swiftly, and behind them a furtive, muffled tumult full of motion and clattering, like the drift of ice in the distance.

Now there was a soft, quick knocking at the window, as she laid her hand on Jürgen's shoulder.

"Yes," Jürgen said, already standing wide awake on the floor, although he did not yet know why.

"The key!" the hunchback called through the open window. "Key to the boat—quick—they're coming!"

Marte asked no questions. She handed out the key. The

distant storm flashed, and she saw the deformed figure pressed against the wall of the house in order not to be seen. The light fell blue on his ancient face. The shadows round his eyes were black like empty wells. When the next flash came he was gone, and his crooked form was crouching dark over the luminous river.

They were growing up all round the house, shooting up out of the light-flecked earth until the circle was closed. Their faces were blackened with soot. They had flails and shafts from the carts and a ladder beam that thundered against the door. Like wolves they stood all round the house, and every flash of lightning drew gleaming outlines round their bodies and flung up a blue shimmering background behind the fury of their gestures.

But everything was mute—movement was without sound. It would have been clearer and easier if they had yelled, if oaths and curses had come flying. But they were mute, and their hatred had the dangerous quality that the hatred of the dumb has, which does not find relief in shouting, but only in the spilling of blood.

"Hold the dog tight!" Jürgen ordered. The panes smashed as a stone flew in. He jerked Marte to one side and grasped the flat oar that stood by the hearth. It made him unsure and hasty in his movements that everything was so quiet. There was only the flashing of the lightning, which came silently casting fire into the room. And it steadied him at once when the dog howled and dragged at its collar as he raised his hand to take the beam from the door. But he had not yet lifted the iron clamp when the house began to shudder under the droning clangor of the plowshare on the other side of the river. Someone was there, hammering at the swinging metal like a madman. Then the sounds tumbled over one another, and instead of the deep, single calls that usually came across the water, there was one ear-splitting roar: peals, one after the other, like bells with desperate men clinging to their ropes, to call all the world together to a place of conflagration, or death, or murder.

This was dead metal crying, but its voice was that of a human being, and the whole vault, lying immense and silent over the circle of the horizon, split at the sound of this voice, and the voice broke out through the cracks in the vault, into the invisible whence a moaning echo replied.

"Heini," Marte said, "he's calling."

The first thing that answered him was a howl of rage round the house. The voice had smashed the silence, the secrecy of the execution. It was as if a sleeper had sat up when the knife was already poised over him.

And now the sleeper came out, shut the door behind him, and held out the oar before him with both hands.

"Men, what are you doing?"

At this moment on the other side of the river the plowshare tore from its wires and fell to the ground. It could be heard quite clearly as it struck against a stone and the swinging metallic note broke off in a whimper, like the sound of a vibrating string that has been cut through. For an instant the wind could be heard passing along the river again, through the reeds, over the alders into the rushes. And once more the heavy voice asked:

"Men, what are you doing?"

The first stone flew. It grazed Jürgen's cheek and banged against the door. The dog gave a howl, and then Jürgen stepped down from the doorstep and began to fight for his life.

He did not recognize any face or voice. But he had no need to. He saw a pack of wolves, and it was all the same whether they had names or not. He knew that he himself was not at stake, but the "white lamb." Somewhere behind these sooty faces hovered the alien face with narrow eyes, like a huntsman behind his hounds. And when he struck out, he felt as though he were striking at the alien face.

Their numbers made them cowardly and awkward. And when they pushed forward all close together Jürgen let the oar whizz around him. Then they fell back and he struck home. It made a dead sound, as though he were striking the body of a heavy fish against the side of the boat. And that was how he saw them, too: pikes' faces, with bared teeth. He was not angry yet, but he was drunk with fighting. The heat and the bitterness of the whole summer were breaking out of him. The smoldering fever of many months rose up and was discharged in the blue light. And he smiled when he thought that she was standing at the window watching him, she whom he had carried in his arms to the bed of love.

He heard her scream even before he felt the knife in his left shoulder. He swung round at the scream and that saved him. Now he could hold the oar only in his right hand, but the joy of fighting went and anger came.

He uttered—a single decisive roar, and it was no longer necessary for Marte to push the door open and for the dog to leap howling at the throat of the man with the knife. It was not necessary for Südekum's panting shout to ring out from the river and his iron ell to come whistling among the "blindworms." Nor for Heini to crouch on the path and hurl stones from his catapult into the scattering crowd, stones that struck among the bodies like bullets. The fight ebbed away, back towards the village—the howling of the dog, the tailor's curses, and the cries of those who had been hit.

But Marte stood in the doorway and watched those who lay on the ground stand up again, one after the other, and drag themselves down to the river. At each flash of lightning she leaned forwards as though looking for someone, but the one for whom she searched was not there. And so she remained standing until Jürgen came back with the others, her eyes peering into the flashes which lifted her white face out of darkness and let it fall back again.

Jürgen was calm again. They washed out his wound and bandaged it. Heini's body was trembling all over, and Südekum called upon the lightning to descend and burn the nest of the blindworms off the earth.

"A nice long stretch of months there'll be," he said, rubbing his hands, "preparation for the Golden City."

But Jürgen shook his head. "No gendarmes, no doctors," he said. "They must go away to America, and if you charge them, they'll have to stay."

Südekum banged his ell against the floor.

"Oh you ferryman of God!" he answered. "They could throw him in the river and he would still lift his hand to prevent anyone telling about it."

"Let it be," Marte said, "as Jürgen says—they won't come again now."

Soon after they had gone and Heini had brought the boat key back, the thunderstorm broke and heavy rain poured down over the land. Marte had not yet gone to bed. She was sitting on the edge of the bed, holding Jürgen's hand and looking out. Thunder was now roaring over river and forest, the room was white, and through the broken window streamed in the smell of the awakening earth.

"Now they'll say they've driven the devil out, Marte. And that God has given them a sign with the rain that they have done well."

She only passed her fingers lightly over his hand, and in the next flash of lightning he saw that she was weeping. She wept with open eyes, without moving.

"Don't be frightened," he said. "They'll soon be going away—rotting water can become fresh again, so why not a rotting village? New people will come, and the earth'll be green again. You have to stand fast in the river, like the saint the fishermen tell of—Christopher—who carried the child Jesus. You'll carry a child too, later, when it's time—now don't cry any more."

'He doesn't know anything about it,' she thought. 'He doesn't know why I'm crying. Oh, he's good and strong. Soon they'll be going away, but first it must be done—one way or the other. So that I can bear a child that won't turn blind in my body. He has the strength to beat a whole village and drive them out, but I need more strength, a different sort of strength—Ten times I've been there, between the firs, and come back again, but some time I'll have to go—soon, before the others go—'

Then she lay down, beside Jürgen in his restless sleep.

The wound healed without a doctor. True, the fever was there in the morning, but he stood up and asked Marte to go into the forest with him. Rain was still falling. They went as far as the edge of a meadow, and there Jürgen pointed to a small, fine leaved plant. Marte had to pick it, because he could not bend so far down to the ground.

"My father," he said, "once got his hand under the ferry cable. They thought the fingers would come off, but he brought me along to this place, and I had to pick it for him. In two weeks he was rowing again. He knew a lot about how the earth can heal."

When they walked back she had to support him. This was the first time he had leaned on her, and in the obscure depths of her soul she felt the full happiness of their love. She had never known much of love. She had seen her father beat her mother when he came back drunk from market, as was customary in the village, and had seen how her mother had defended herself with everything she could lay hands on. Then she had discovered that she was desired and that it was sweet to give way. But this had been what Jürgen called "the desire," a sensation of ecstasy dying out quickly in bitterness.

But now she was walking beside this man who was a giant and a child, who would put his hand under the ax for her, who had scattered a village and now had laid his arm around her shoulders so as not to fall. They stopped by the dead field which Jürgen had not yet plowed. The stubble had been scorched by the summer, and the stone seat shone darkly in the rain. From every twig it dripped into the loosened earth. They stood under the last tall pine and heard how the forest rang in the rain. It was still the mating season and a buck drove his doe across the field, past them. They heard the high, half mournful, half luring call of the driven animal, wandering here and there through the thickets and fading away over the crackling of twigs. Jürgen looked away, towards the village, as if he had not noticed anything, but she put her arms round his neck and pressed her body close to his.

"You shall have a child, Jürgen," she said softly, "just as I promised. Soon you'll have it, and it will stay with you, for ever and ever— When they've gone away you won't need to wait any more."

At home she laid the herbs on his wound and the next morning the fever had gone. He would not stay in bed but sat outside the door, his hands folded idly for the first time in his life, and watched the clouds passing over the moor and the swallows gathering and the grass growing up again. Meanwhile Marte cleaned the house, as through Easter were coming any day now. She scrubbed and washed and polished all through the house, even the attic, picked up every object, set it down in its place again, looked through the clothes, the chests and the nets, fetched glass from the shed and fixed the broken window-panes, and from early morning until evening she worked as though she were preparing for a festival or making everything ready so that she could hand over her duties to another and stand before her master without reproach.

"Why are you having such a turnout?" he asked. "It's still a long time to go till Christmas, isn't it?"

But she smiled, looking past him across the river. "It must all be clean and tidy," she replied, "after all that's happened."

And then Jürgen got into his boat again and began to fish. The nights with the falling stars came, and the first evening mists. The late, scanty harvest came, the days grew shorter, and the jays came down to the fields to see if the early potatoes were dug. A motorboat had come from the town and unloaded its supplies, and a letter from the burgomaster and the sheriff had come, in which the ferryman and fisher Jürgen Doskocil was thanked for his neighborliness and his good deed. And the pastor had come and brought three fruit trees and planted them himself and sat with Jürgen for a long time by the ferry, talking with him. But Jürgen had shaken his head. No, he did not want any punishment for them. If God's heaven were a court of judgment, then they would all come out of it badly, and as long as He did not charge them Jürgen had no right to play the beadle.

And one day very early, when Jürgen was about to go down to the water, he found a little boat of birch bark lying on the doorstep, clumsily and rather lopsidedly hollowed out of thick bark, with the tip of a peeled willow wand for a mast and a scrap of white cloth for a sail. It was such a boat as he had carved for the children in the summer, when they lay in the forest and forgot their hunger as they watched the jackknife in his hands.

He bent down and lifted it up cautiously. In the bottom of it lay a mallow blossom, just the head pulled off the stem, as children pick flowers. And looking at this boat Jürgen forgot all the bitterness of the year. He smiled again for the first time since the battle in the night, and went back and put the present in the middle of the table, by Marte's Bible, so that the mast stood upright and the white sail shone, friendly, over the black binding.

Chapter Seven

AND ONE DAY HEINI CAME AND TOLD him that the papers had come, the entry permits and the tickets, and that today there was to be a great gathering, and on the fifteenth of September the village would set out for America. And, oh yes, a free ticket had come for him too, because his mother had made a secret arrangement with the American, and they would have to kill him before he would go to America with those who had received grace.

Neither of them noticed that Marte rose and went out. Nor did they notice that she moved her joints carefully as she walked, as though they were stiff and frozen. Only the dog stood up slowly from the fire and followed her.

She went slowly down to the river, stepped onto the ferry and sat down on the rim so that she could lean her back against the cable and fold her hands in her lap. She liked to sit here when Jürgen was on the water. Here she could see down the river, and when she half shut her eyes she could imagine that the darkly drawing current would gradually lift her, together with the ferry, and glide out gently, bearing her away—just as a cloud, slowly changing, dissolves and is no longer there.

When she sat on the other side of the ferry and looked upstream, everything was unquiet and difficult and dangerous. The light fell on the river differently, each eddy could be seen as it came, and it seemed as though all the water were ceaselessly pouring down into her and she would choke like someone drowning, her mouth full of water.

The sun was low over the moor, dark red, without sharp edges. The river water glowed, and the bushes and stacks of peat on the moor cast long shadows so that she pulled up her feet and covered them with her skirt. Children were calling to each other in the fields. A blue, warm smoke rose from the early potato fires into the still air, and on one of the oaks by the house a late woodpecker was knocking.

She sat quite still and quite unfolded and let all this sink into her. She had known nothing of the earth but that it was hard to dig one's bread out of it, that the pastor might talk of sowing and harvest, but that one's back ached when one sowed and harvested. She knew that the sun burnt and the rain drenched and the frost hurt one's hands when one lifted out the last turnips. And that the forest and the earth might be beautiful to the squire's wife as she sat in her carriage, but that one learned to know only the hardship of forest and earth if one grew up among work and poverty.

But now, in this hour, on the brink of everything, she knew that this countryside was beautiful for her too. The river and beyond it the moor, the forest and before it the fields. And she knew that it would be hard to leave all this and go away—from Jürgen and the river, the dog and the flowers at the window, the sun over the moor and the smoke over the fields. She knew that all could be well without the child. For after all there were Grita and the dog, and the finches that fetched grains of corn from the doorsteps. And Jürgen was there, a whole kingdom of joy and delight. Let the beasts of the forest bear children and bring them up, because no one was there to put spells on their children and make them blind in the mother's womb. But why should she go, first to the firs to kneel there, and after that further, to kneel again? Had an animal to kneel in order to have a child? Where was her sin, that she had to kneel?

She turned her head a little because she heard the engine of a boat upstream. Yes, that was the boat from the town. In the morning it had come by, decorated with flags, a band on board and many people who had waved up at the house. They had been celebrating a festival and now they were going back. But they did not know what was happening here. No one knew, not even Jürgen. Only she knew. There she sat on the ferry, with folded hands, quiet as a woman asleep. But her hands were spinning. No one could see it, but she saw. They were spinning a gray thread, which unrolled along the gray wood of the ferry and piled up, and the red sun turned it red—

The boat came round the bend. A girl's voice was singing, softly accompanied by plucked strings—*Five young birches once there stood—birches young on Mamel shore—sing, sing what happened there—they found the bridegroom nevermore—*

Again she turned her head slowly and watched it all gliding down into the field of her vision: the white wave before the bows, the flags, the dresses, the faces. 'If the boat knocks against the ferry cable,' she thought, 'then perhaps it'll throw me into the river—they'll scream, but they won't find me, because I shall hold on to the weeds at the bottom, like the water birds when they're wounded—' But the boat slid past the cable, and they waved to her with handkerchiefs and drinking glasses and hands. They probably knew that she was the ferryman's wife. She would have lifted her hand in answer, but she could not tear it away from the thread she was spinning. She made an effort and her eyes stared full of fear at the rapidly passing boat. She opened her lips to cry out, but she could not. Now it had reached the island of rushes, then there was only a blue flag on a mast, and then it vanished behind the alders.

Soon after that the rim of the sun finally disappeared behind the moor, and a cool light flowed over her from all sides. The ferry swayed slightly in the boat's wake, and two thin white streaks of foam ran murmuring along where the boat had passed. Then that too faded out, and the first heron dropped on heavy wings out of the evening sky, into the reeds. The dog stood up, looked at her once and went slowly back to the house. And then she was quite alone, above the dark water and under the evening star that stood small and white above the sunset.

From this evening on Heini disappeared. They searched for him in the forest and in the river, but no trace of him was found.

His mother said that she would beat another hump out of him when he was found, but even so they did not find him. And then the people began to pack up their goods and chattels for the Golden City.

At the end of the first week in September, in the dusk, Jürgen came back from the town where he had delivered the fish. The waxing moon stood over the water before him, and dark loose clouds were going slowly over the white sickle, in a warm wind. Then the earth darkened, without becoming quite dark, and the moon broke out of a rift in the clouds, as though it were traveling. It was an unquiet changing, and in all the shapes of earth, the reeds, the alders, the edge of the forest, a swaying light fled and returned, veiling itself and then appearing again where it had been.

Jürgen did not like this light. It dazzled and confused him, and he had to row back round an island of rushes once because he had missed the mouth of the river. The town had seemed noisy and malevolent to him, and over his eyebrows was a dull pain that he knew and feared. He looked round from time to time, slowly turning his head over his shoulder; but nothing could be seen but water, a far bank, a solitary light.

Where the river passed between the fields of rushes, on the straight course from the town to the mouth of the river, he suddenly saw that his feet were in water. He bent down and dipped his hand in: there was no doubt that there was water in the boat. He steered the boat into the rushes to keep it steady, reached out for the scoop and began to bale the water out. An obscure uneasiness filled him, but then he thought that the boat had been lying in the sun the whole day and it was possible that the tar had loosened and a joint had warped. Yet he baled hastily although he saw there was no danger.

The water fell from the scoop into the reeds with dull splashes and the noise of his work depressed him still more. He let his hand rest and raised his head. The reeds were whispering in the wind, a fish leaped somewhere out on the river, and then every sound faded again, swiftly vanishing away to the rim of some enormous circle where it held its breath. 'Stuff and nonsense,' he thought, and bent down again to the floor of the boat. And as he bent he saw that someone was sitting opposite him on the seat—a dark cloak, a shadowed face, and bare feet showing white through dark water. A cloud was over the moon, but the figure was there.

Perhaps it did not last longer than the space between two rapid heartbeats. But in that space Jürgen recognized that it was Maclean. And Maclean was bending down to the floor of the boat like himself, and staring at his white feet. His right hand hung in the water, as though playing, and his left held the wide, shallow hat pressed to his chest. No chill radiated from him, no horror. He sat like a traveler whom one has taken on board and who, sunk in thought, idly gazes into the river.

And then he was gone, and the moon came out and lit the gray wood of the seat.

Jürgen baled out the rest of the water, knelt on the wet floor, found the crack between two boards and stuffed in one of the rags that always lay under the stern seat. He waited a while longer to see if it would hold and then pushed out of the reeds into the mouth of the river. Now the landscape seemed as quiet and orderly as usual. He smelled the withering alder leaves, the reeds, the last whiff of the potato fires hanging in the sheltered creeks. He looked at his hands; they were steady as ever, and the pain above his eyebrows had gone. 'Like an abscess, the way it gathers,' he thought, 'and then it breaks open and it's all right—' Only his feet were cold and in his knees was a dull feeling as if they had been bent too long.

When he came round the last bend, he saw Marte kneeling at the ferry, washing her hands. "She could do that at home," he thought, "it's not good kneeling over the current."

But then he leaned forward without thinking and watched her. He was too far away to see her face distinctly. Only her movements were visible in the moonlight. Over and over again the body bent forward and dipped the hands into the water, and then the hands were lifted, cupped together as though to hold the water they had scooped up. But it flowed away between the fingers, and then the hands brushed up and down against each other, as though they were trying to get rid of the very last drop. And then they were lifted into the moonlight, as though to be carefully scrutinized, and suddenly, with something like a shudder, they were plunged into the water again.

At first it looked quite natural, although somewhat weird in the uncertain light. But then the unwearying, rigid evenness of the movement became uncanny, as if something were rising and falling on the current, and Jürgen suddenly began to be afraid.

But when he plunged the oars into the water with a sharp blow, Marte held her hands still, as though she were listening, stood up slowly and went calmly up to the house.

When he stepped out of the boat he felt once more that his knees were tired, and again he thought of the apparition. But even now it was only like a dream, without horror and without the wavering chill that usually hovered behind every vision of the second sight.

Marte had already gone to bed. There was no light in the room.

"I heard you coming," she said. "Have you had supper?"

Yes, he had had a meal in the boat before he started.

"Then come to me," she said. Her voice was hushed and calm, but something about it puzzled him. "She spoke as though she were already asleep, and the voice came from far away: not from her body, but from a long way off behind it, like a voice calling in the dark from a lake, when it is impossible to tell whether whoever is calling is in a boat, or swimming, or standing on the farther shore.

He paused in his undressing and leaned forward a little in order to hear better, but her breathing was quite calm and her brown arms lay quietly side by side on the white pillow.

"You mustn't sit by the river any more," he said, "the water's too cold and anyone can see you when the moon's shining."

"The dog was there," she answered in the same voice. "Come to me."

Again the voice went through him, cool and strange, and suddenly everything seemed altered: the room, where light and shadow mingled, his bare feet in the light on the floor, the chair where Marte's clothes lay neat and tidy, the shoes in front, the stockings over the back, the Bible on the striped shirt. They were her Sunday clothes, and again he was puzzled.

"Has anyone been?"

"No, nobody."

He frowned, with slow, heavy thoughts that rose like bubbles out of dark water, laid the beam across the door and then went to the bed which stood in the shadow. A white streak of moonlight lay between him and the bed, and again he looked at his feet as he passed through it. How white Maclean's feet had been, as though they did not belong to him and really ought to be brown, or still darker like his cloak.

Marte shifted slightly to one side. She was lying on her back, her arms still side by side on the pillow. It was all as usual, but when he had covered himself and lay still, suddenly he heard her heart beating. He raised his head cautiously and listened. At first it was only his own blood, but then he heard distinctly how her heart was thudding. He turned on his left side and slipped his arm under her head, but before he could say anything, she put her arms round his body, laid her head on his chest and said softly:

"Now I want to have the child, Jürgen."

He felt how she was trembling, ceaselessly, but then joy overwhelmed him. Everything that had happened during the day plunged down into a whirlpool and everything else, her voice, her heart beating, her trembling, was now clear and without mystery. She wanted to have the child—He had not understood anything, the washing in the waxing moon, her voice, and how she had said 'Come to me!' Never would he understand anything until it was said to him, like that, across his chest: 'I want to have the child, Jürgen.' And he put his big hands on the crown of her head and kissed her on the temples, which were moist as with cool dew.

Jürgen did not know how long he had slept. The moon had moved on. Its beams now fell on his face pouring white light into his open eyes. At first he thought that he was on the river and that the reeds were stirring and whispering on his right. But then on his right someone spoke, a familiar but far, remote voice that seemed to come from the lake and to pass through him like a cool breeze.

"You must get up, master," the voice said. "We must go to town."

He shut his eyes again, but the rustling went on, and he realized that it was Marte putting on her clothes.

Then he was standing on the floor boards, wide awake, looking at her.

"What's the matter, Marte? Why aren't you asleep?"

But even while he asked, he saw her face, a white, set stony face. The features were the same, but behind them was a different being of whom he knew nothing, who was looking at him out of a stranger's eyes and went on repeating: "We must go to town—don't let me go alone, master—there I shall speak—don't ask—dear master, don't ask—"

There was a break in her voice, such a broken sound that Jürgen hurried into his clothes. But he threw them off again and took his Sunday suit, which hung behind the curtain. She was ready first and sat waiting on the chair, with shoes and stockings as at their wedding, and she held the Bible in her lap with clasped hands, beside the bundle she had knotted out of a red kerchief.

She stroked the dog over the head, telling him to stay there, and left the door open behind her. And then they left the place. She did not want to go by water. She wanted to walk the same way that she had come that time, and then through the forest beyond the moor. It would be four hours journey, but as she wanted it so Jürgen did not argue. The moon was already low in the sky, mist hung over the hollows, but no bird yet called over the moor. The air was warm and still, and in the oak wood early ripened acorns were dropping to the ground through the withering leaves.

Marte's face had lost its rigid look. She breathed deeply, and now and then it seemed to Jürgen that she was smiling to herself.

"May I hold your hand, master?" she asked in a low voice.

"Why do you say 'master?'"

She looked at him from the side, for a long time, with sorrowful meaning in her eyes. "It may be," she replied, "that my service is at an end now."

"Marte!"

But she only repeated her question and then took his hand.

He was carrying her bundle on his stick, over his shoulder, and so they walked along the dewy road side by side. Never before had they walked like that, hand in hand, in the silence of early morning, with no work to do and wearing their Sunday clothes. It was like the walk to a wedding, and although to Jürgen all this was still like a bad dream, he felt that there was something of greatness and wide space in this dream. Never in his life had he taken such a walk. He would have liked to lift her up in his arms and carry her to the town, because in the night she had become a mother and because she seemed frail and sweet as a flower. Something had happened of which he knew nothing, but it would turn into a blessing. She was good and a saint, standing at his river like the chapels in those countries where there is another faith.

They would walk for an hour, and then sit down for a while on a tree trunk or a milestone, and Jürgen would take his coat off and fold it neatly with the lining outside, so that Marte need not sit in the dew. At the first stop she took off her shoes and stockings because she was not used to walking so far in them. He looked at her brown feet with their fragile angles, and love for her filled him so that it was like a pain in his heart.

During this first rest she began to talk, quietly, almost gaily, like a child, and it was her childhood of which she spoke. She told him about the few dolls she had had, and about the dog Karo which had only one ear, and the teacher, and the goats she had had to watch. And how they used to sit in the fields in the evening round the last potato fires, and how the moon rose over the forest and they sang songs so as not to be frightened. "Now dusk falls over the heathland—homeward we will go—" That was the song she had loved best. And about her father, who drank, and her mother who made her kneel on peas when she had broken a cup. But there was no sadness in these stories, only a cheerful turning back into the past, as though she were gliding in a boat back the same way she had come up on foot, laboriously along the banks. And as though she were singing to herself very softly as she went.

And now she talked too while they walked. At first of her confirmation time and how she had been very devout. And her old pastor was still alive and she would greatly like to see him again. And she told him about the curate too, whom she had loved, and that it had always been difficult for her to carry love for God in her hands as a pure spiritual love. She had been too religious and once, when she had got a hard beating at home, she had wanted to run away and be a nun. The Spiritual Bridegroom, that had been such a beautiful expression. And then, when everything visible had been finished with the Communion, she had become different, lightminded and not good, and she had given much love in order to find the ground for her anchor, as it said in the Bible. But she had not found it that way, and she felt she was not worthy of his love, however much she had washed in the river.

He looked straight ahead along the road, which now ran bright between the brown autumn woods.

"Once you came to me," he said in a low voice, "in the night. Not for the sake of desire, but in the mercy of your heart. And for the bare feet on which you came, all the other ways you went are forgiven you—not in my eyes, but in yours, for how should I be the first?"

She pressed her hand tighter into his, and when he turned his head he saw that now something had thawed from her face, the frozen look had become soft and melting. But he saw too that it was not merely a changing back to the face he knew, but a transformation beyond that into a new face that he did not know yet.

Yes, and then the new faith had come, and the bad thing about it had been that it contained the visible, the Golden City and—yes, much more as well. And so she had jumped in as into a well, with her eyes shut. And so she had been when he first knew her. And that had been bad too, for he had leaned over the edge of the well and looked at her, and then she had felt how cold it was in the well, and slowly, very slowly, he had lifted her up. But the other thing had held on to her and so she had almost been torn apart. And then she had cut it through, once and for all, else she would have fallen for all eternity, and that was all, just that.

Again they sat on a milestone. They had gone round the moor, and the sun was rising on their left. Fields and meadows were sparkling in the dew, and over a hill stood the town's church spire. The cross on top flashed in the sun like a star. The larks were still there, and wild pigeons were gathering on the harvested fields. To the right, in the distance, a flock was passing along a dusty road, and the shepherd's horn sounded with many echoes from hill to hill.

"You must sow rye, master," she said, "this year. They'll be gone, and no enemy will come to your field."

His face was becoming more and more heavy with grief. Still he understood nothing, except that something grave and solemn was happening.

"You won't say what it is?"

"No, master, I must only say it in the town. Have patience with me. And I know now what you must call him. Innozenz you must call him. The pastor says it means 'he who is without guilt,' and that is what you shall call him."

Then they sat down once more, on the last milestone

before the town. She put on her shoes and stockings, and it took a long time for her to tie the laces. Her fingers were uneasy, and while he looked at her hands, he thought that they looked as if they had been in the water for a long time. The skin seemed so pallid and bleached.

She did not let go of his hand, but now she carried the bundle herself. In the streets the people gazed after them, not only because they walked hand in hand, but because their faces looked so strange between the gray of the cobbles and the houses.

When Marte crossed the market square towards the county court building Jürgen began to tremble. He felt her hand growing cold in his big, warm hand, and she pressed his fingers as though there were a great pain somewhere in her body.

"Be calm, master," she said softly, "please be calm."

But he could not help it that his whole body shook, and it took some time for them to reach the top of the steps.

Yes, the magistrate was there, but they could not see him. What was it about?

"A thing has happened," Marte said, "and I'm sure he will have time for it."

The sergeant looked at her attentively, and suddenly his expression changed. He had seen many faces in his life and he knew what this kind of blank shimmer in the eyes meant, seemingly passing through everything, not to be diverted or subdued.

"Is something wrong?" he asked, lowering his voice.

"Yes, something's wrong," Marte answered slowly.

They were led through a wide double door. Jürgen wanted to stop there, but Marte was still holding his hand and walked along with him to the big table by the windows where the magistrate was sitting.

He had a small, smooth face, brown and unwrinkled like a piece of cloth. But his eyes were big and gray and gentle, as though they did not belong to this face but to another second face living hidden behind the brown cloth.

"You want to make a statement?" he asked, and his voice also was gray and gentle. "Who are you, please?"

"My name is Marte Doskocil, father's name Grotjohann, wife of the fisher and ferryman Doskocil—here—and I declare that yesterday evening I killed the preacher of the Mormon church, Maclean, with a knife."

She put word to word, slowly but without pausing, in a hushed, remote, slightly husky voice. It was as if the voice were behind a wall of mist and were speaking into it. And when she stopped, everything sank away, and only the wall of mist stood motionless in the room, and the three pairs of eyes that were trying to see through it.

Then Jürgen's heavy stick fell to the floor. It fell with a single dead knock on the linoleum, and in this one sharply cut off sound lay something inevitable, a final confirmation that could not be changed.

Yes, she wanted to tell everything. The clerk of the court came in, a gray man with stiff hair who looked as if he had spent his life under a stone. They were both given chairs because they had walked for four hours, and then Marte began. She still held Jürgen's hand, but she did not look at him. She looked straight ahead into the magistrate's gray eyes, and only out of the corner of her eye could she see Jürgen sitting upright on his chair as though he were made of wood, staring through everything, probably right to the cabin behind the firs, where the dead man was lying white and stiff on his camp bed.

She began with the calling to grace by Maclean in her home village.

"Please spell it," the clerk said. The magistrate interrupted her and rang up the gendarmerie. Yes, such and such had happened, the officer on duty was to go to the village immediately, to the cabin of the preacher Maclean, and see that no one entered the place before the investigating officials arrived.

Marte continued. She told of her move into Jürgen's cottage and how Maclean had followed her. And that he had desired her as a bride of the church who was his due, and that he had cursed the fruit of her womb for as long as she would not do his will. And of the breaking of the ice and the stillbirth of the child. And from then on she had believed that he had power over her womb. She had not been able to tell anyone, for Jürgen would have strangled him. And she told of the Shrove Tuesday night, and the oats, and the attack on the night of the storm. And of his hand, which reached out for her over Jürgen's head. And of the hollow between the firs, where she had knelt without finding strength. And of the child that Jürgen wished for and that she could not have because it would have been blind.

The pen scratched and ran on. Jürgen still sat as though made of wood. The magistrate had his head resting on his right hand, his gray eyes fixed on her.

"Then Heini came, the hunchback, and said that the papers and the tickets had come. There was only a fortnight. And then only a week. Then he would have gone away and the curse would have stayed with me. Yesterday Jürgen was in the town. At dusk I went there. I had the knife in my bodice. I prayed by the firs, and then I went in. Yes, in a week he would be going. The curse? No. 'That's not a curse,' he said, 'that's a prayer.' I knelt before him, I embraced his feet and kissed them. No. I was to undress and lie with him, then he would stop praying. I said he must swear, and he swore it—on the Bible. I put the knife away secretly and I did it—I had no strength for the other thing—I—yes—when I wanted to go away he asked when I was coming again. He wanted to take the emigrants to the ship and come back and live in the village. And three times a week I was to come to him, else he would pray again. I had the knife in my bodice again, here. He was still lying on his bed, and I drove it into his heart. He was dead at once. I locked up after me. Here's the key."

She unknotted the red kerchief and laid the key on the table. She remained standing, looking through the window out onto the market square.

"It's a sin," she said then, "and I'll pay for it. But they must let me live long enough to bear Jürgen's child. It's his child that I'm carrying, his alone, and he will christen it Innozenz, for that means 'he who is without guilt.'

"Innozenz?" the clerk asked. But she did not answer.

"Yes," the magistrate said after a long pause and looked at the key. "You will have to stay here now, Mistress Doskocil. I think that the judges will deal mercifully with you if everything was like that, but—"

"They shall judge me an eye for an eye," Marte said, "as it is written, but they must wait until the child is born."

"Nothing will happen to your child," the magistrate said, and then he nodded to Jürgen.

Jürgen stood up. When there was danger he understood everything, and he knew that now she would go away for a long time. He went up to her at the table and very cautiously laid his hand on her shoulder. She swayed under the light touch, so weak was she now, and he know of nothing else to do but to lift her up as he had from the water that time and hold her to his chest.

"For me," he said, "you did it for me. You saved me from doing it. I shall go to the Minister, to the President, they shall let me do penance for you—you're a saint, like those that stand by the rivers, in the chapels—"

She laid her cheek on his shoulder and closed her eyes. Everything loosened in her face and in her body while she was listening to his words; the tension passed from her forehead, her eyelids, her mouth and arms.

"No, no," she said like an eager child, "only I can put it right, Jürgen, only I myself. But afterwards, then everything'll be good and new, won't it? The field and the child and life—won't it? You'll keep me, won't you? And—listen, Jürgen—I swear to you, now, here, that it's your child, do you hear? Only yours—I know that—from before—Do you believe me, Jürgen?"

Yes, he believed it and led her to the door, and the magistrate went out with her and nodded to him to stay.

They went in the motorboat belonging to the inspector of fisheries. They talked nicely to him, each of the gentlemen, and told him that there would not be a heavy penalty. And he nodded, but everything about his movements was even slower and heavier than usual, as though something in him had been broken and only a thin joint were holding the broken parts together. And besides, he had to look at the water and at the place in the reeds where the other had sat before him with white feet.

They shook their fists at him and shouted, all the village, and the magistrate had to give an order for the gendarmes to draw their truncheons. They found everything as Marte had described it. The knife was still sticking in his heart, and the police doctor said after he had made an examination, that the rest was true too, about the violation. On the floor, carelessly wrapped in greaseproof paper, lay the photographs, and the pastor recognized five girls from the village among them.

In the big parish council room the investigation took place. The girls denied nothing. There were no contradictions or obscurities, only the blindness of fanatical belief. There was no accomplice, no one under suspicion, no one guilty.

They carried the corpse to the boat and went away.

The thudding of the engine could be heard a long time afterwards in the still September air.

The pastor called the parish council and all the villagers together and told them what had happened. Sin had been committed by the dead man and by them. But now they were to take it as a sign that a curse lay on the road to the Golden City, and they would do better to stay and give up the false prophets and their teaching. But they stared sullenly at the floor and kept silent and looked at their sticks, and the first one whom the pastor asked for his opinion said that he had no time and must pack for the great journey. And after him the others pushed their way out, and only the young people remained behind, who were not going and would now have to hire themselves out as farmhands.

The pastor was a heavily built man, in body and in soul, and all passions would bank up in him for a long time as behind a sluice, before they broke out. But now he raised his fists and shouted:

"Well then, go to the devil in the devil's name!"

And it was no good his being sorry immediately afterwards and blushing for shame.

He leaned heavily on his stick and walked slowly along the path to the ferryhouse. There were no curtains at the windows in the village any more, and no flowers. Crates and baskets stood in the yards, and the dogs crept about the street with their tails between their legs, because they knew they no longer had masters. It was the pastor's twentieth year in the village, and he walked through the midst of his harvest with eyes cast down.

Jürgen was sitting on the ferry and the pastor sat down beside him. The water gave way under their heavy bodies, and so they sat there as though looking a little uphill, not at the shining surface of the water but at the tops of the young alders.

"Two sinners, Jürgen," the pastor said and felt at once that his joke was out of place.

But Jürgen had not even heard.

"They all tell me," he said as if he had been talking for a long time already, "that they won't keep her for long. And that's good. But even the good is not the right. If you meet an adder, pastor, then you beat it dead. And you don't get punished. Why should she have to stay there in the gray building?"

The pastor drew circles with his stick on the rough wood of the ferry.

"When you start arguing and brooding," he said, "then it's all up. You see, if the village takes you for an adder and kills you, then they get punished because they have taken a human being for an adder, and a human being isn't one. And if Marte were to come along the river now and say that she had been set free, then you would be happy and she would be sad and uneasy all her life long, she and the child she is carrying. For whoever sheds blood must do penance so that he can become happy again."

"Uneasy, yes, that might be true, pastor."

"Ah, Doskocil, there's only one fool sitting on this ferry and that's not you. Twenty years I have plowed my furrow here. Just look at the harvest." He raised his stick and drew a half-circle round the village.

"No, pastor, it's the same as with my oats. Should I kneel down and tear the stubble up? If the oats weren't for me, then the rye will be for me, or the potatoes, and if that comes to nothing as well, then perhaps it is God's will that young trees should grow there again. You've got to try things and not be afraid."

The pastor stood up. "Thank you, Jürgen," he said, with a little smile at the corners of his mouth. "Now we both know what we have to do."

The village emigrated. But no cart traveled over on Jürgen's ferry. They all went the long way round to the next bridge, and Jürgen saw only the cloud of dust on the road and now and then a child's face looking from the top of one of the loaded carts over towards the river where he was standing. And in the night he was wakened by the dog's howling. A red glow filled the room, and when he stepped out of the door he saw that Maclean's cabin was on fire and the last rafters were plunging into the flames in a shower of sparks.

And by the time the ship must have gone he came back from the water one evening and found Heini sitting on the doorstep. His clothes were torn to rags, there were still withered leaves in his hair, and his face was pale with hunger and exhaustion; but there was a smile on his twisted mouth. Yes, he had been in the forest until it was time, and now the ship was out on the ocean.

"They've taken me back," he said, jerking his head

towards the village, "and when you need me, just strike the iron twice and I'll be there."

The trial was held in October, and the proceedings did not last longer than an hour. Marte was sentenced to a year's imprisonment, and she did not wish a petition for mercy to be made on her behalf.

"I killed so as to have a child," she said. "That is mercy for me, and I don't want any other."

But Jürgen asked for one favor. He stood up from his bench and walked up to the judge's seat. His face was gray, as though it had passed out of the world, and his arms hung down at his sides like something that did not belong to him, but he looked the judge fearlessly in the face and said in a loud voice that he wished to ask for the privilege of carrying his wife and the child she was to bear into her cell as he had carried her out of the water into safety. For he too wanted to have some part in what she had taken from his shoulders.

For a moment there was an embarrassed, uncertain silence, because his simple words made justice, however leniently it had been administered, no longer clearly distinguishable from injustice. And the foreman of the jurors, a big fishery owner, a man who was very sure of himself, got up and walked to the window, as though he did not want to see any more of all this. Then Jürgen was permitted to do what he had asked, and he took Marte gently in his arms and carried her out of the courtroom as though no people were around him but only a silent forest where he walked warily between the trees so that her tired feet should not brush against the bark.

And she kept her eyes shut like a child shielded from harm.

In the afternoon Jürgen returned from the town. It was a calm, gray day, and the calling of the wild geese could be heard far and wide. The forest looked like green grass and Jürgen dipped his oars quietly because at every sound the withered leaves seemed to fall from the trees on the banks. But it was not cold. Everything was merely hushed and drawn close, and the little peat fire on the moor was not like a fire in the open country but like a flame in a hearth between quiet walls.

Jürgen thought how he must plant flowers in the spring, so that next autumn when they came home, Marte and the child, there would be something bright and gay about the house. For him it was good as it was, with its grayness and quietness, but for her there must be something to which her tired soul could cling, something like a nail for a traveler's coat. He thought of mallows and of asters. And besides that he would paint the house —white, with green beams. And he would carve a little windmill and set it on the fence for the wind to play with even when everything else was still.

But between all these thoughts, which passed slowly and radiantly through his mind's eye, other pictures came again too—the corridor, the staircases, the doors. And the gray, narrow room that he had never seen before where she would now live, her small face and her firm brown hands, and the place where she would rest them in the night, when no one was there. And when he had made the boat fast and walked up to the house, he was like a gray wolf wandering through an empty forest.

Heini was sitting on the doorstep.

"I thought we'd have to plow today," he said. "I've got everything ready. The oat stubble's still there, and it's time for the rye to be in the ground."

At first Jürgen gazed past him, with empty eyes into which everything sank without a trace: the hunchback, the house, and the field. But then he nodded and went into the room to change his clothes. He trod as softly as though someone were asleep there in the big bed, and he looked sideways at the hearth. But there was no one sitting there.

And then they did the plowing. The hunchback walked behind the plow, and Jürgen pulled his weight in the broad harness. The dog scratched up mouse holes and pushed his nose into every spoor. The forest was gloomy and silent, and only the faint rustling of the clods walked along with them. When they had turned the plow to start a new furrow, they rested a while. Then they could hear the last acorns dropping in the yard.

They spoke no word, plowing until twilight. The field was small, and when the sunset hung over the moor they had finished. The field lay dark and moist and a thin mist hovered over the fresh soil. Jürgen only nodded, and the hunchback slowly disappeared over the fields.

The dog stood waiting at the corner of the forest, but Jürgen did not go yet. He still had the harness over his shoulders and one hand on the handle of the plow. He looked into the sunset and the red glow was in his eyes, but not its meaning. From the air and the vast silence he could feel that he was alone, but he also felt the fresh earth under his bare feet and how its coolness rose up through them, as in a tree. He stood very still, as though wishing to grow there, and he felt it climbing higher and yet higher, a strong and humble sap striving towards his heart.

And he saw a field with green blades that gradually turned yellow and bowed under ears of corn. And he saw a child lying among these stalks, asleep, while a man and a woman were cutting the corn and binding it and setting up the sheaves.

So he stood until the thin mist over the fresh earth rose still higher and enfolded him yet more closely. And then he was like a tree, soundlessly drinking the dew of the night.